PILATE

BY

ALEX CRISTO

InAmerica Press

Published in the United States by InAmerica Press

a division of InAmerica, Inc.

POB 2645, Valley Center, CA U.S.A.

InAmerica and colophon are registered trademarks of InAmerica, Inc.

Library of Congress Cataloging-in-Publication Data

ISBN 978-1-934613-43-6

Cristo, Alex, author.

Pilate

Alex Cristo

First U.S. Edition

[First Printing]

InAmerica Press website address: www.inamericapress.com

Printed in the United States of America.

ALSO BY ALEX CRISTO

For my parents and brother.

IUDAEA ANTE DIEM III NONAS APRILES XXX

(Jerusalem, 30 A.D. April)

PATRIAM IN VIA

It was cold and blue outside the walls of the barbarian city of Jerusalem. The orange sun was still a few hours away from rising. The Roman governor's procession of soldiers and attendants moved slowly and lethargically, guided by large golden standards and torchbearers. The torches glowed and the dark coal smoke reached into the sky. The soldiers and advisors easily followed the torches at night as they let their minds go numb for the long, arduous march. The standard they followed was that of Pontius Pilate, the fifth prefect of the Roman province of Judaea, Commander of its Legion, and representative of Emperor Tiberius Caesar Divi Augusti filius Augustus.

Every year, for the past ten years, the prefect and his administration were demanded by protocol to make the exhausting two-day journey from Caesarea to Jerusalem. Caesarea was a port city and the administrative center for the Roman's rule over the barbarian region of Judea. It was built in the Roman style with a deep harbor port, theaters, sports arenas, baths, and markets. There was a Roman aqueduct to bring water into the city and the markets were full of rich trading items from across the empire. It was the closest thing to a proper civilization in this wretched land for those not fortunate enough to live near Rome.

Jerusalem was the capital city of what the barbarians called Israel. The Romans captured the city 100 years earlier without even unsheathing their swords. The Jewish people simply let Pompey the Great into the gates. To the Romans, it was a filthy city in a small province on the very edge of the empire with no real political importance. The governor, to his shame, wasn't even given a legion to command, only auxiliary troops – an extreme slight to a governor who had led several military campaigns in Gaul. He still referred to the auxiliary troops as his legion though.

Governor Pilate's legs were sore and he was irritable. The grating sound of metal armor scraping together rattled his mind and the dust cloud kicked up from the road caused his throat to ache. He was forced to ride a horse instead of traveling in a carriage as the roads were so terrible and poorly maintained that riding in a carriage caused the prefect horrible waves of nausea. He hated riding the military horses they gave him. They were large, stupid brutes that wanted to bite and slam their heads into anything they saw. They hadn't the grace and breeding of Pilate's personal horses, but he wouldn't dare ruin his stock by subjecting them to such terrible conditions.

Although it was dark, Pilate knew there was nothing to see. The road to the city was only rocks, weeds, and dirt. The entire countryside looked like burnt bread. He hated this festival and the logistical nightmare it caused with troop movement. In the days leading up to the Jewish Passover festival, Pilate had stationed most of the 3,000 auxiliary troops under his command in and around the city.

EXTRA MURUM PORTAS

Jerusalem was a walled city with eight main gates. Pilate and his administration entered the gate in the western wall. Pilate called this the 'palace gate' because it was immediately north of the palace he used when he occupied Jerusalem. Someone had told him what the Jews called it a long time ago, but he had forgotten. He had no ear for other languages, especially barbarian tongues. He also struggled with his Greek and had no recognizable sense of humor about this deficit.

As they entered through the square limestone gates, Pilate accepted salutes from the station agents. Inside each gate was a customs station where publicani collected taxes on all goods entering or exiting the city. During the day, many agents were stationed, but at nighttime only a few were required.

The formation traveled south along the road that hugged the city wall. The city was so crowded for the Passover festival that thousands of Jews had taken to renting spaces on the roofs and steps of the stone houses. To him, they looked like animals and beasts – disgusting, dirty little things that offended every sense and sentiment. If all these barbarians were just a piece of cloth, he thought, I would tear them into tiny shreds.

Pilate and his entourage continued into the palace's main gates. When they passed the first defensive tower they turned into the main gardens. The bulk of the soldiers broke off and traveled towards the barracks. The Roman governor was escorted into the large courtyard by his personal armed Roman guards. Their faces were still covered in darkness, but the path was illuminated by smoking torches held by troops and servants. The pre-morning light reflected off the silver-colored armor like blue splashes. The procession was led by two gold standards of Caesar Tiberius. They were long poles topped with statues of golden eagles and images of the great emperor engraved into them.

Standards were a symbol of Rome's dominance. While Pilate occupied the palace, it was his duty to place the standards outside the palace and throughout the city. This was a proclamation to the people that the prefect, and the might of Rome, were now within the city walls.

As he dismounted his brute of a horse, it tried to bite him again. He shoved the horse's big head with his fist and stretched out his legs as he walked up the stone stairs. A captain saluted as the governor casually raised his hand and walked by.

The soldiers placed the standards prominently outside the entrance to the palace and then the governor and his entourage followed the soldiers inside. Pilate coughed and rubbed his parched throat.

As the prefect and his escorts arrived at the governor's praetorium, they were met by his 'legion' commander. The commander and the five military men accompanying him raised their right hands up to the sky and saluted. "Hail Caesar."

The commander was a large, rough-looking man with hawkish features and a calm intensity.

The governor returned the salute to the guards around him. "Report," he said.

"Governor Pilate, we are ready to place the standards in the street at daybreak."

Pontius Pilate turned to the commander, revealing his fatigued face in the glow of the torch. "Do it now," Pilate said. "Before they wake."

"Yes, sir."

Pilate casually returned a salute and glided up the stairs. His robes rose like a crimson curtain against the cold stones of the stairs.

The Roman soldiers placed golden standards throughout the city. These tall poles were topped with the gleaming gold cult images of Emperor Tiberius. The deep colors of the Roman symbols stood out in the rustic, traditional setting of the Jewish city. The standards were now the only graven images representing the human form in the entire city. The red flags attached to the top of the poles would snap in the wind and they would be easily noticed against the sunbaked stone of the ancient city.

ALIO MODO NEGOTIUM AGERE

Iovius rode his mule towards Jerusalem. Hordes of people were massing to enter the city outside the main gates. Even though he was a Roman, Iovius still had to wait in the queue. He hated being forced to wait. I'm a Roman citizen, not some beggar, he thought.

Posted outside the walls, silhouetted against the sunrise were the rotting corpses of crucified men. They lined the main road to the entrance on both sides. The smell of rotting bodies was almost unbearable but Iovius barely took notice; it was a commonplace sight on this far edge of the empire.

Crucifixion was the Roman's cruelest and most hideous form of torture. Prisoners and dissidents would be stripped naked and scourged. The scourging would consist of a Roman soldier using a whip to remove skin and cut deep into the body. The blood and fluid would flow out of the prisoner and embody the grizzly spectacle of pain.

The prisoner would then have to carry a wooden beam through the city, naked and bleeding. Everyone in the streets would have to endure and witness the humiliation and horror. Usually the condemned would have a titulus, a small board that proclaimed the prisoner's crime. Then, the prisoner would be bound to wooden crosses. Hands and legs were nailed to olive wood. Often rope was used when there were not enough nails but Governor Pilate never ran out of nails. He would send troops to pull them out of boats and wagons before he used rope. He never wanted to diminish the experience and spectacle for anyone.

Men and women would remain on the crosses for days, sometimes weeks, rotting to death. They were forced to publicly endure exhaustion, thirst, and starvation. Once their suffering had been prolonged for as long as humanly possible, their bodies would begin to decay and peel away. The bodies would ultimately be consumed by wild animals and denied a proper burial. By any and all standards, it was a horrific way to die. It was efficient, cruel, and systematic. It was thoroughly Roman.

Crucifixion was also a necessary tool for Roman foreign policy. Most cities occupied by Rome adorned such decorations by the main entrances. Iovius and anyone who walked past tried not to look at the horror. In all honesty though, it simply couldn't be helped. Those emaciated mangled bodies, the terrified white eyes. No one could pass by without looking and feeling despair. It was a rotting forest of dread and terror.

Iovius rode through the street of Jerusalem with his small caravan of slaves. He was on the bottom step of the Roman equestrian class. Although his station was above that of slaves, freed men, foreigners, and commoners, he was still below the senatorial class and other equestrians.

He had camped outside the city for days waiting for word that the prefect had entered the city. When he saw the standards posted outside the walls and along the streets, he knew the governor was in the palace.

As Iovius passed by the gold standards, he saw groups of Jews in outrage over them. At first, he thought they were drunk, but they seemed too angry. They were cursing and yelling. They were ripping their clothes and slapping their chests. Iovius was amused at such extreme behavior. What strange customs these barbarians have, he thought. How amusing.

Iovius arrived at the palace. His slaves dispersed and took his mule to find the stables. There were a large number of Jews gathering in a courtyard. They had torn clothes and angry faces. They were very unsettling and growing in numbers. Iovius realized that today may not be the best day to speak to the governor about business matters, but he would have to make do. There may not be another chance and he needed to act presently to secure his business prospects.

Hardalo, a palace servant and slave to Pilate, approached Iovius with a bowed head. The servant wasn't permitted to bow to any Jewish visitor. However, he could see by the way Iovius was dressed that he was indeed a Roman. The quality of his clothes and the number of servants with him suggested he even had some rank attached to his name.

Iovius' slave approached Hardalo and held up his arms in a traditional posture.

"This is Iovius of the Domitius, equites equo publico and personal friend to the governor," the slave said.

Hardalo saw that Iovius wore the narrow-striped tunic and gold ring that was indicative of his rank. This was the lower station of the knightly classes but not a true member of the knightly order. His rank meant he could not hold public office or join the upper orders, but it did mean he was owed a certain amount of formality and consideration. Any Roman citizen was entitled to use this rank if he had taken part in a census and met the property requirements. Iovius just barely met the property requirements. He had obtained his wealth and rank through rigorous travel and merchant dealings, much to the derision of the men of quality in his order. He was now bound to his travels and most of his acquired money went to keeping his rank. In order to keep the wealth quota for his title, he was forced to continue trading. He was able to afford his eleven slaves, but it was nothing close to the 500 slaves that served Pilate.

"The attendant will take your slaves and mule to the stable. If the eques would follow me, I shall take him to the reception area," Hardalo said. The entire time he spoke, he had his head lowered. He hadn't seen a member of the knightly class, even a low-ranking knight, in almost four years. It was rare to receive people of quality this far away from Rome.

Iovius was impressed with the governor's slave. He had a shaved head and carried himself like a military porter. His walk was unassuming, but not wilting. He stood up straight. He was small and thin, but appeared deadly, like a wild dog. A very high-quality slave.

Pilate and his advisors were organizing the logistics for the coming festival. He had changed into his white Egyptian-linen toga that was rectangular and draped around his body and over his arm.

His toga was held in place partly by keeping his left arm pressed against his body. His equestrian tunic, which he wore under his toga, was completely white with a thin red stripe down the ends.

Tradition allowed for male citizens to have one piece of jewelry. Most men of Pilate's order wore a personalized signet ring that was used to make an impression in sealing wax as an authorization for documents or as a key to a personal lockbox. Pilate's ring was gold, but a bit on the small side for the governor's taste.

The advisors crowded together in a courtyard under the sun. Pilate had a boy holding a shade over him to keep the hot sun off his balding head. Although he was a competent administrator with better than average rapport with his staff, he was tired and a bit overwhelmed by the most important Jewish date: the Passover.

The festival always got in the way of troop deployments and border conflicts with the Parthians.

"The Parthians have redirected their troops along the border," the commander said. "The legate of Syria demands you send three cohorts to the border to bolster defenses."

"I can only send one from my legion. We have to keep the majority here, one stationed at Caesarea and the others at their current positions. The Parthians aren't going to attack."

"The legate thinks they are planning to prod the defenses."

"The Parthians don't prod. They retreat. Have you heard of their battle tactics?" he asked the commander.

"No."

"Their horsemen ride into battle and draw the enemy forces up a hill. As the opposing forces climb after them, the riders turn around as horses continue to retreat and fire arrows. They can fire arrows at their enemy while they retreat."

"That would be a big advantage."

"Only if you are used to running from the battlefield." Pilate laughed. "When I was in Gaul, we always let the beggars run if they wanted to. No need to chase them. All they run with is the stink of defeat and fear. One cohort. If they do cross the border, it will only be a few dozen men on horses to stir up talk for their recruits."

The attendant, Hardalo, entered and addressed Pilate. "Sir, Iovius of the Domitius, equites equo publico has arrived."

Pilate perked up with excitement. "Is that right? Very good," he said. "Gentleman, I will greet our guest."

The advisors acknowledged the governor and bowed as he turned away from the table. They continued with their work, happy to see him occupied with something else.

Pilate approached Hardalo and stretched out his stiff neck with his hands.

"When did he arrive?" Pilate asked.

"Presently, sir," Hardalo said. "I am seeing to his people. I have him waiting in the garden for you."

Pilate was followed by Hardalo into the garden. Iovius stood by the pool admiring the local flowers and décor.

"Iovius!" Pilate called.

"Beware the Greeks, even when we bring gifts," Iovius said smiling.

"You don't bathe enough to be Greek and you don't have the money to bring gifts."

The old friends shook hands, hugged and kissed each other's cheeks.

"I am Greek!" Iovius said with a smile. "My father's grandfather was half Greek."

"If you want to make that claim, I certainly won't keep you," Pilate said.

"Are you ill? You look like a battered door."

"Your humor escapes me," Pilate said.

"If you batter a door, it becomes misshapen and the color is uneven," Iovius explained.

"Please, let's leave the writing and composing to the Greeks." Iovius was about to protest but Pilate raised his hand. "The full Greeks."

The commander of Pilate's personal guard entered and saluted, out of breath. "Sir, there is a mob gathering outside."

"Is that right?"

"They want the standards removed from around the city," the commander said.

"Let them gather all they want. When the sun becomes hot and mealtime comes around, they will cease to care." Pilate dismissed him with a wave of his hand and the commander trotted off.

"What is this you are wearing?" Iovius asked, bending over slightly to view the fabric from the side. "Wait until you see what I've brought you. Some very wonderful things from the east."

"Such as?" Pilate asked.

"I've brought you silk from India and Egyptian linen. I have also brought some wonderful spices; cinnamon and ginger. I have brought oils from Athens and Spain.

"Oils from Athens," Pilate said, marginally interested. "Spices and oils; you *have* brought gifts. I suppose you are here to sell me something."

"Don't be so stormy, you'll ruin my wonderful mood," Iovius said.

"I apologize, that was most rude," Pilate said. "Why are you here?" he then asked, knowing Iovius had come to sell something.

"I've come from Lycia. I'm renewing some trade relationships. Once it was known I was traveling out this far I received satchels of correspondence for you."

Iovius produced a leather bag and began to hand Pilate letters and messages. "Here is one from your sister, one from your old advisor. Oh, and here is one I was told to give you first. It's from the Regent."

"Is that right? Is there some other horrible wasteland they want me to govern?" Pilate said sarcastically.

"Wasteland? This is a very nice town. A little town, for sure. I must say I'm surprised. It has a certain, barbarian magnificence, doesn't it?"

"Inexhaustible," Pilate said as he went through the process of opening and reading the letter.

"I am amazed at how large the temple is but the roads are crap."

"Don't get me started on the roads," Pilate said, raising his head in exasperation. "It's all I can do to keep my troops stationed and fed at the borders."

"Troops? Who would want this land?" Iovius asked.

"The Parthians."

"Never heard of them."

"Greek and Persian descendants. Your people, as you say. One of Alexander the Great's generals. Theater lovers, with their domes and schools. They educate their woman you know."

"Savages," Iovius said.

"The Parthian king writes Greek poetry and wears makeup into battle."

"How theatrical. Are they good warriors?"

"Nothing to a Roman. However, they do have an interesting cavalry," Pilate said as an aside. He was charmed by the tactical advantage of firing during a retreat. "Their Parthian king married his mother and took her as his queen," Pilate said with disgust.

"Is it true they mutilate their genitals?"

"I have no idea, I've never met one."

"No, the Jews."

"Oh yes, everyone who enters the city must. I'll send for yours to be done at once," Pilate said as he read the message. Iovius couldn't tell if he was serious. "What brings you to Jerusalem?"

"I was on my way to see you in Caesarea, but I heard you were to be stationed here for another week."

"Yes, every year I must descend into the land of the goats and watch over these little bleaters during their temple festival. Do you have business in Caesarea?"

"I was hoping to establish new and profitable trade relationships."

"That's a great distance for trade relationships," Pilate said.

"No distance is too great for trade," Iovius replied. "I was hoping, based on our friendship, you could give me a letter of introduction to some business patrons in Caesarea."

Pilate set down his letter and rubbed his eyes. He knew he would be forced to listen to another business proposal.

"What is your prospect?" Pilate asked as he let out an annoyed sigh.

"Caesarea is one of the main ports on the trade route to Egypt. Now, Egypt is, of course, the main supplier of grain and wheat to Rome and the empire. Ships are constantly leaving the port of Alexandria in Egypt and traveling to Rome with hulls full of grain. But when they return to Egypt, for the most part, they're empty. These shippers are on the seas and half the time their holds aren't earning them money. So, from Ephesus to Myra to Tarsas to Caesarea, the holds are empty. And there is where the opportunity lies.

"Things that are exported to Rome are expensive. Olive oil, wine, and wheat take up the bulk. If you want to export other goods you have to find boats. All the reliable ones are already chartered for olive oil, wine, and wheat. Imports are already locked up by the big families.

"If I'm an owner of one of these boats, I'm not doing as well as I could because I only make money when I go towards Rome with grain, not when I leave with nothing—"

"Sir," the commander said as he entered the room. "The crowd has doubled in size and they are becoming agitated."

"Very well, I'll have a look," Pilate yelled. He was becoming interested in Iovius' business proposal and very annoyed at the interruption.

"A priest from the temple and an emissary of Herod are with them, sir."

Pilate was shocked. He suddenly took the situation seriously. Why would an emissary and a high priest gather with an ordinary mob?

"Very well, excuse me, Iovius. I'll have to read this message you gave me when I get back." He handed the letter back to Iovius and then walked towards the courtyard.

"May I come?" Iovius asked.

"By all means, you can observe me administer spankings to the barbarians." Pilate's voice echoed off the walls of the corridor. The rising sun cast an orange glow on the hallway's stones and mosaics.

The commander had remained still and waited for Pilate to walk ahead of him and then for Iovius to follow. Pilate and Iovius strode through the corridor with their arms clutched to their sides, keeping their togas up. The commander whispered orders to attendants and messengers.

"Now, commander, if the case may arise, we should post a couple of soldiers in reserve," Pilate said confidently. "Tell the men we don't want a situation, we just want to show we have the force."

"Yes, sir, I'll see to it right away." The commander ran ahead of the group.

"In reserve. This all sounds so exciting," Iovius said.

"Calm down, they're just children testing their limits."

"Can I speak to them?" Iovius asked.

"No," Pilate replied.

"Can I hold a spear?"

"No."

VULGUS VESTIBULUM

Pilate emerged into the brilliant sunlight at the top of a two-story elevated terrace overlooking a courtyard. His hand rested at his temple, shading the sun. Pilate's translator stooped behind him next to the commander and his lieutenant. Iovius leaned against the back wall of the terrace, watching with excitement.

The translator took his position next to Pilate's left ear. The translator's father was a Roman soldier and his mother was a local girl. Apart from his commander, he was actively hated by Romans and Jews alike.

Iovius was shocked to be faced with scores of angry Jewish eyes. The crowd was screaming and reaching for the governor in exaggerated gestures of lamentation.

"What are they barking about?" Pilate asked. Pilate's white robes gleamed in the sunlight.

The translator strained to listen to the crowd. He leaned close to inform Pilate. "They're upset about the placing of the standards of Caesar throughout the city. They are offensive to them and violate their tradition. A terrible blasphemy," the translator said.

"Tell them to be silent. I am about to speak," Pilate said. Pilate looked at Iovius and rolled his eyes.

The translator relayed the message, but the crowd did not quiet. The rumbling grew louder as a small group made their way to the front. The two white-skinned men that led the group were dressed very well, their clothes adorned with jewels. The two men presented themselves.

"He says he is Boaz, Herod's administrator," the translator said. "The other is Caiaphas, the temple's high priest."

Pilate hated Boaz and his eyes blazed at the emissary.

"I know who you are," Pilate said. He turned to Iovius. "This is what I was talking about, those two both speak Latin and Greek, but if they speak to me in Latin, the Jews can't understand. This whole thing is for the Jew's benefit. They are showing off for these commoners. They are children." Pilate looked directly at Boaz and Caiaphas. "Children. I know you can understand me," he said bitterly. "Why are you here?"

Boaz and Caiaphas spoke.

"They want the standards removed," the translator said.

"Is that right? Tell them, as a representative of the emperor, the standards go where I go," Pilate said. "If they don't like it, they can simply leave the city. When I leave after the festival, the standards will go with me and they may return to the city free from offense."

The translator relayed Pilate's words. Boaz and Caiaphas then spoke to each other.

"See that one, the one with the green on his tunic?" Pilate said to Iovius. "That is Boaz, the emissary to Herod. And the one there, all in black. That is Caiaphas, the high priest. Mongrels. Appointed by my predecessor. And here they are, two servants at my door demanding something of me. My servants! Making demands! Mongrels."

"They say, do not cause a revolt. Do not cause a war. Do not break the peace. Disrespect to our ancient laws brings no honor to the emperor. Do not make Tiberius an excuse for insulting our nation. Tiberius does not want any of our traditions done away with. If you say that he does, show us some decree or letter or something of the sort so that we may cease troubling you and appeal to our master by means of an embassy," the translator said.

"Is that right? Appeal? An embassy? Did these swine just issue a threat? To me!" Pilate's superior attitude suddenly transformed into insult and anger. He turned his head and nodded towards the commander. "How many troops do we have available?" Pilate whispered.

"Only a handful."

Pilate nodded, intimating that he wanted troops to be issued around the crowd. He knew, though, that four guards wouldn't be enough to intimidate a crowd this large. "Get us more," he whispered. "No swords. Only clubs. We can't have any deaths."

The commander retreated into the palace and began recruiting troops from other posts.

Boaz spoke.

"They say it isn't a threat, just procedure. They also say it might be difficult for the embassy to explain the logic of some of your accounting- and peacekeeping capabilities. They gave a slight reference to being corrupt and brutal, but not in an accusing way. It was very subtle; I couldn't really understand it," the translator said.

"No, I understood that part." Pilate's angry eyes became so large he could use them to swallow the crowd. He turned and saw the commander had returned. "You beggars should go back to your pathetic lives or I'll have to show you the power of Rome."

The crowd continued to yell and gesticulate towards him.

"Commander! Engage!" Pilate yelled.

The commander screamed out an order. Fifteen Roman soldiers sprung out from the sidewall. They had silently moved into position wearing cloaks while the crowd had been focused on Pilate. They were armed with clubs and whips. They began to ruthlessly beat and savage the men in the crowd, careful to not draw any blood or hit any vital body part.

They clubbed and punched and kicked every man in the courtyard. One soldier came upon Boaz, King Herod's emissary, and stopped. The soldier didn't raise his hand to him as they had been told not to hurt the emissary or the high priest. Pilate knew any attack on the aristocracy, even of a barbarian culture, wouldn't look good in a report.

Pilate watched the men beat the crowd. He looked on like a general evaluating the readiness and effectiveness of his troops. He oversaw his troops like he had done countless times before during his campaigns in Gaul. He had some critiques for the commander at their next meeting. Pilate loved moments like these as his men could practice and use it as a discipline exercise to stay sharp and motivated.

The soldiers had dispensed Roman justice on the crowd with their clubs with great effectiveness. The only people who were left standing, that weren't Roman, were Boaz and Caiaphas.

"Do you see what you force me to do to your commoners?" he said to Boaz. "Now get out of my courtyard or I'll have each of your throats cut." Pilate knew he couldn't actually kill them. He had been warned several times before by his superiors that he couldn't kill without discretion. He needed to show restraint and cause. His superiors, Pilate thought, didn't have the battlefield experience he had and didn't understand how necessary it was to show proper Roman strength, even without cause.

The soldiers were ordered to stop, and they formed ranks in front of the terrace below Pilate, awaiting further orders.

"Do you wish to remove yourselves or shall we continue?" Pilate said.

The beaten and bruised men of the courtyard helped each other up.

"Continue," Boaz said.

There was a cold silence among them. Pilate was confused. They weren't afraid. They were defiant. They gathered together and faced the governor. Pilate shielded the sun from his face so he could better see what the crowd was doing.

Pilate realized that Boaz knew he had been reprimanded for being brutal by his superiors. The governor was under orders to keep from using the soldiers on the population. This crowd knew they were going to be beaten, Pilate thought. They are daring me to kill them. They know it would risk my post.

Even though Pilate held rank at the fringes of the empire, he was a low-ranking aristocrat, and was certainly looked down upon by the Roman elite.

The governor couldn't think of a counter to the Jew's stratagem. He dropped his arms to his sides, releasing the toga down his arm. The careful folds and creases bunched together as the weight of the white garment fell into itself. He could only retreat into his palace.

Pilate's head was spinning as he entered his palace. He stomped and tripped over his toga.

"Commander!" Pilate screamed.

"Yes, sir," the commander said, jogging towards Pilate.

"When the sun makes them hot and thirsty, they'll disperse. When they do, I want you to send someone to follow Herod's emissary. I want a report on what he does. Do you understand? And if any Jew so much as touches one of the standards, I want his head beaten in, is that understood? And, recall more troops from the city and have them posted here at the palace, we might need them.

"In fact, if anyone approaches too close to the standards, I want him beaten. And you arrest that barbarian emissary. I would like a word with him in private."

"Yes, sir." The commander sprinted away.

Pilate stomped down the corridor like a spoiled child sent to his room. Iovius walked next to him.

"What silly business!" Pilate screamed. His legs and arm became tangled in his toga and he began to stumble. He thrashed about, throwing his toga to the floor.

"That was quite a spanking you gave them, very impressive," Iovius said, laughing to himself.

Pilate turned and pushed him like an angry child. Iovius stumbled back and overturned a vase on a table.

"Mind your tongue, you beggar. And don't walk next to me. I am a governor, you merchant." Pilate continued down the corridor. "You have no idea how tasking this job is."

Pilate took his robe and threw it across the corridor, erupting into a larger tantrum. Having remembered why his merchant friend had arrived, he quickly stopped. A new source of income may be useful if the tax collections were short for the Passover. He collected himself, adjusted his tunic, and turned back to help up Iovius.

"Forgive me, Iovius. This is an especially difficult time for me." Pilate held onto his arm as they walked together. "These barbarians are stubborn and froth at the mouth over the slightest thing. Do you know how hard I had to work to get my commission for this post? How much money I had to pay? Now you were speaking before about a business opportunity?"

"Yes," Iovius said carefully. "I was hoping to discuss it with your permission."

"This is the Jews most important religious festival. It commemorates their freedom of slavery under Egyptian rule. You can imagine how a festival that celebrates revolt would be a tender situation for a Roman province and the Roman governor that is responsible for it."

"What are you going to do?" Iovius asked blankly.

"I'd love to burn the whole bloody city to the ground."

"Sounds expensive."

"Yes! Expensive. You are exactly right. You don't understand how expensive it is to be in my position. All shortfalls in taxes are considered against me. I have to buy support in Rome and with my superiors. If anything, it is a full-time job to outmaneuver these barbarians that you just saw. They constantly try and undermine me and go behind my back.

"Herod is the worst of them. He's been collecting taxes off the peace I provide and buys support in Rome. I don't know how that barbarian has been able to buy more support than me. He somehow convinced my superiors to reprimand me for being violent. As if they knew how difficult it was to keep these people in line and paying on time. It is impossible to fully conquer a people with an invisible god. Commander!" Pilate screamed. "Where is the commander?"

Hardalo rounded the corner and bowed his head. "He is coming, sir."

"And Herod, that mongrel. You can almost respect the people; they just respect their god and traditions. But Herod not only thinks he's Roman, but he thinks he is my equal."

"What is his rank?"

"Herod Antipas is the son of the former client king. He is formally in charge of the rural countryside known as the Galilee. He is a pig. My equal! He's that mongrel that married his mother. Or his sister? Hardalo!" Pilate screamed.

Hardalo bowed.

"Is Herod married to his mother or his sister?" Pilate asked.

"It was his dead brother's widow, sir."

"See, I was right. Incestuous barbarian," Pilate said. "Now, about this prospect you have. We should discuss it. Shall we have a bath?"

UT INTER BARBAROS LOQUI

The commander took the translator with him to a side hall and shoved a bundle of dirty clothes into his chest.

"Put this on," the commander told the young man.

The translator removed his Roman tunic and put on worn clothes, similar to what men wore in the city. He was petrified. He knew he was going to be ordered to do something dangerous. He was going to be asked to leave the entourage and go outside the palace walls. The land outside the palace walls was occupied by Jewish people and Roman soldiers. Both looked upon him with contempt as he had a Roman father and a Jewish mother. He was hated by everyone as an outsider and would be at their mercy.

"I want you to make your way through the crowd and try and listen for any useful information," the commander said.

"They'll tear me apart, sir. They've just seen me translating for the governor."

"No, they won't recognize you. It's difficult to make out men's faces on the terrace. It's far away and too sunny."

"Yes, sir."

"If anyone spots you, quickly get out of there. They might tear you to pieces. Otherwise, stay there until sunset. Take this." The commander gave him a small dagger to tuck into his belt. "In case something goes wrong."

The translator left the palace through the side entrance and walked a couple of blocks away before turning back. He wanted to approach the crowd from the street rather than from the palace.

The temple hovered over the city like a thunderstorm. The tall white stone walls and smoke from burnt offerings dominated the city's landscape. The buildings and roads were made of limestone that seemed to glow in the sun, and the streets were busy and crowded with frenzied activity. The population of the city grew to six times its normal amount due to pilgrims from all over the countryside coming to the temple for the Passover festival.

In addition to the agitations from the overcrowded conditions, the people in the street were noticeably upset and offended by the Roman standards placed throughout the city. As everyone woke up to graven images of a foreign king placed in prominent areas of the city, they were indignant. This wasn't just disrespectful; it was considered a sacrilege.

The indignation was most visible outside the governor's palace. As the translator entered the courtyard, it was clear everyone instantly knew he wasn't a Jew, though he didn't know if they recognized him as the governor's translator. If they recognized him, they were smart enough not to say or do anything about it. Everyone turned their back to him hoping he would go away, cradling their battered arms and heads. They were hugging and holding each other, shaking from their frightening assault.

The translator had seen many instances of people from the city reeling from their dealings with Roman soldiers. Usually it was a bloodier affair with many casualties. He listened to the harsh words they directed towards the Roman palace. They believed that because they were speaking in Aramaic, the Romans wouldn't understand them. The translator laughed. The Romans knew the Jews were cursing them, they just didn't care.

He made his way through the crowd with his ears straining to hear any useful information. Even if they are pretending to accept me as a common man, he thought, they are not going to say anything for me to report back.

It was easy to spot Boaz and the high priest. Their clothes were not worn, they carried themselves like men of quality, and neither were bruised from the recent assault. Boaz and Caiaphas were surrounded by agitated supporters looking to them for leadership and direction. Everyone was yelling and shouting and waving their hands in the air. Boaz and Caiaphas were flanked by temple guards and attendants who were trying to keep the others at a respectable distance.

After a few words of encouragement, Boaz and the high priest removed themselves from the hot courtyard and fled to the cool shade of a covered passage. The translator was able to stand around the corner and listen. He didn't appear to be eavesdropping due to the distraction of all the men around him yelling and waving their hands and attending to their wounds. The translator pretended to rub his neck and arm in an attempt to blend in with the beaten crowd.

"That business was unnecessarily dangerous," Caiaphas said, wiping the sweat from his head. They spoke away from the crowd in Greek. They thought neither the Jews or the Roman soldiers would be able to understand them.

"Don't be ridiculous. We won," Boaz said confidently.

"No, you bought a larger defeat for your next engagement. Once you and Herod are finished posturing and maneuvering with the governor, I will be the one he reconciles his wounded pride on."

"Are you worried the governor won't appoint you for another term as high priest?" Boaz asked, implying that the high priest might be a Roman collaborator.

"Even your master, King Herod's power, is at the pleasure of Rome," Caiaphas said bitterly.

"No, it is the people that he reconciles his pride on," Boaz said. "Now the people have more respect for you. Pilate can't bully you if you have the people's respect."

"That is precisely why he would bully me. Or they can declare the temple as nursing a rebellion and destroy it. They can sentence the Jewish people to death or slavery."

"You are too paranoid, old man. Do you know how much money the temple brings the Romans? Pilate needs the temple more than you do, high priest. Once Herod is the king and administrator to Rome for Judea, we can return to our traditional way of life."

"So, we should trade one gentile ruler for another?" Caiaphas asked.

"Mind your tongue, priest. Careful who you insult."

"There aren't enough Jews to fill the ranks of your foreign and civil wars," Caiaphas said. "We are a minority in our own land.

More and more, Jews are going to Greek theaters and Roman baths. They are going to the agora. They aren't going to synagogues."

"Herod doesn't want soldiers, he wants subjects," Boaz replied. "Let the Romans worry about the wars. They control the borders and keep out the invaders."

"You really have me in a difficult situation. You have shown public disrespect to the Roman governor. He is, most likely, planning to have me killed at this moment."

"No one forced you to be here," Boaz said.

"If I don't show solidarity with your stupid outrage, I'll lose authority with the people. But I suspect that was your plan all along. You are playing a silly game here. Our culture is dying. More people are learning Greek than Hebrew. You are risking the necks of the Jews in your battle with the Romans. Your king is too ambitious," Caiaphas said.

"My dear Caiaphas, the very money you pay him builds temples and graven images in Rome to be worshiped. You already have no authority."

"Better they are built by our taxes than our own temple stone and blood. We have plenty of walls to defend the temple. But the walls do nothing from those on the inside."

"It was Jews who let Pompey and the Romans inside the walls," Boaz replied. "Besides, soon we won't need the governor. We are already preparing an embassy to meet with his superior, the legate of Syria. All we have to do is wait for him to raise arms against the Jews in the city and cause a riot and we can have him removed."

"You really think you can do that? The Romans call you a barbarian, do you think they will accept an embassy from a barbarian to depose of one of their governors? Are you really going to sacrifice tens, perhaps hundreds, of Jewish lives?"

"Better to risk hundreds than lose thousands," Boaz said casually.

"The Romans are excitable and childlike by nature; you can't continue to antagonize them," Caiaphas said.

"They are fools and bullies," Boaz responded.

"They are most certainly not fools. And all you have to do is keep irritating them and they are liable to close their fists tighter around us," Caiaphas said.

"You are such a well-trained lap dog."

"And you are a fool. Our temple was destroyed once. They just need the smallest excuse to set fire to this one. You and Herod have kingly positions. Our people only have our traditions and our temple. And as of right now, we are able to keep both. We are a minority in our own land," Caiaphas said. "You inciting Pilate will just bring his replacement, or worse yet, the legions. Do you really think that confronting Rome will give your master kingship?"

"They don't want to live here amongst us. They want to take everything of value and leave ashes. Leave Rome here long enough and there won't be any more Israel."

"If you keep antagonizing them, there won't be any more Jews either."

"Do you think we should keep the Roman standards of Caesar posted around the city?"

"No! It is blasphemy," Caiaphas said. "But I don't want scores of Jews to be slaughtered again."

"You don't want to lose your palace either."

"There is a better way to get him to remove them. Slapping him in the face outside his palace isn't one of them. If you had not made such a show of it, I could have appealed to him in private to take them down."

"Pilate is cruel and brutal. Even for a Roman. I'm sure the people would be much happier with a half-Jew king who respects their ways than a hairless Roman who wants all Jews dead. If I had to guess. It sounds like you are too comfortable with the way things are," Boaz said.

"What are you talking about?"

"You have a remarkable residence."

"It is the personal residence of the high priest."

"And you are a high priest. And you have your own personal mikveh bath?"

"What of it?" He gazed angrily at Boaz.

"Hail, Ceasar," Boaz said, raising his arm like a Roman. He smiled and returned to the corridor.

"I want you to take these men you brought with you and run back to your palace. You are going to get us all killed. I will go talk to the governor, try and calm them down," Caiaphas said, following him.

"I can't, most of these people I didn't even bring with me. They are here because of the standards. No, this is great. I'm going back to join the crowd; they need a leader."

"Don't antagonize them, you fool. Just let the Romans be or you're going to get all of us killed. The Romans aren't going to let a barbarian king speak for them. No matter how Greek he acts."

"Don't worry, high priest, I will be sure to let the governor know that you preferred to cower in your own residence."

Boaz reached out and lightly placed his hand on Caiaphas' arm. Caiaphas pulled his arm back, immediately offended by Boaz's touch.

"You aren't permitted to touch a high priest of the temple," Caiaphas said.

"You aren't a high priest. You're a collaborator. I doubt you are even Jewish. Run along now."

The two hostile men glared at each other. Caiaphas lifted his hands into the air and walked away. Boaz entered the courtyard again. He was instantly surrounded by the battered men. He began to give them comforting generalities and continued to issue inciting hostility towards the Roman governor.

The translator had an impulse to follow Boaz into the courtyard but stopped himself. He feared he would be immediately discovered as a collaborator. He knew the Jews and Boaz would be able to see he wasn't one of them. He wouldn't be Roman or a soldier or a Jew. He would be a Roman collaborator. A half-breed Roman collaborator. The worst thing to be in Jerusalem. He would be torn apart before he could call out for reinforcements; reinforcements that wouldn't come anyway.

Instead of returning to the courtyard, the translator followed Caiaphas through the streets. Caiaphas was quickly flanked by two temple guards who carried spears and ushered people out of the way. The translator followed them from a distance through the streets. The temple guards were not gentle in creating space for the high priest to walk.

The high priest lifted his black cloak as he walked, careful not to get it dirty. The front and back of the cloth were made to be as one. They were made of blue, purple, and scarlet linen, and the sash around the priest's waist was intertwined with golden threads.

Over the cloak, the high priest wore a breastplate. Fastened on the front of the breastplate were twelve precious stones in four rows of three. Each stone was engraved with the name of one of the tribes of Israel.

Caiaphas was eventually led through the large arched gates and into a courtyard. Temple guards were stationed at every door and wall. Visitors were talking and waiting. The two guards hurried past them and into the main corridors that surrounded the inner plaza.

The translator did not dare follow. The large walls were well fortified and heavily guarded. He hadn't realized the Roman appointment of the high priest was so comfortable.

Caiaphas was throwing his hands around and yelling. He hated dealing with the Romans and King Herod's advisors. He needed a bath. He held his arm stiff and walked towards his inner residence within the complex. He descended two flights of steps into the cool air of a damp chamber. He waved off attendants and guards as he rushed by them.

Caiaphas entered his mikveh and closed the entrance with a thick heavy drape. The small pools were used for ritual cleansing and were built to strict specifications set out by Jewish law. According to the Mishnah, the earliest rabbinic code of law, they had to be of a certain size and filled with 'living' water. The water could not be transferred from a vessel but needed to flow directly into the bath from a river, spring, or rainwater collector.

Caiaphas' body was pale and hairy. He had not worked a day in the sun in his entire pampered life. His skin was rough with many scratch marks and sores. He descended the steps into the cool water. The water from this pool was connected to a pipe which was filled by large jugs of regular water.

As he descended the steps into the pool, Caiaphas reached down and grabbed a small hand-sized porous stone. He bent his knees until the water was up to his neck. Then he took his stone and began to scrub his body. His pasty white skin became red and streaked. He spent extra time scrubbing his arm where Boaz had touched him.

Caiaphas placed the stone back on the first step and got out of the pool. He descended another set of steps through another doorway. The lamplight from the wash pool barely illuminated the small room.

Built into the ground were two waist-deep pools that held two hundred gallons of rainwater. The pools shared a common partition that had a submerged hole between the basins that were two inches in diameter. The free exchange of waters between the two tanks made the waters of the immersion pool an extension of the natural rainwater, and therefore permissible by Jewish law.

Rainwater was collected from three large basins that were carved out of the stone on the roof. From there it flowed, without any interference from man, into the large tank. The walls and floor of the pools were paved with plaster, adhering to the Jewish law that water from a mikveh is prohibited to seep into the earth.

Caiaphas stepped into the mikveh pool and submerged his entire body. He stepped out shivering, his skin tingling from the scrubbing. He would not be able to enter the temple until he was ritually pure, which he now was, a state that was difficult to achieve after dealing with the Romans.

CALIDUM BALINEUM

Pilate let Iovius enter the apodyterium first. They approached the small entrance that contained niches to store clothing. Pilate and Iovius stripped off their togas and tunics and placed them in the wooden holders.

The governors before Pilate had converted part of the palace into a private bathing facility for their private use while stationed in Jerusalem. Pilate had been looking forward to his bath since he woke up.

They proceeded into the frigidarium, a small rectangular room with vaulted ceilings and the first of three chambers. A round shallow pool made of waterproof concrete was located by the back wall. The tile on the floor was weathered and stained. Pilate descended two steps into the pool and submerged his entire body and head. Iovius followed suit. The pool was barely large enough to fit both the men. They cupped water over their heads as they spoke.

"This one is too small. The one at my residence in Caesarea is much nicer. This just keeps me from going insane in this stupid city," Pilate said. "See, it's falling apart." He grabbed at the bottom of the pool and picked up some mortar that had dissolved. "I'm glad I only have to be here for this ridiculous festival."

"What is this festival?" Iovius asked.

"It celebrates the Jews liberation from Egyptian rule."

"When was that?"

"Who knows? Long before the Romans and the Greeks and the Trojans. Now they use this festival as a passive way to keep hope alive that they will one day rise against the might of Rome. Little beggars, as though we couldn't see through their little ruse."

"I didn't know the Egyptians ruled Judea?" Iovius asked.

"No, they were slaves in Egypt and their god set them free and sent them here, to this wasteland."

"That's a long way to travel. There's a large desert in-between isn't there?"

"Very large. But who understands the will of the gods?" Pilate said sarcastically. He was fed up with the notion of gods, both foreign and domestic. He had never seen anything to convince him of such nonsense.

"How did their god do this?"

"By making the frogs kill all the first-born children."

"That sounds terrifying."

"I know. These sneaky little barbarians think they are being so clever. This entire religious festival is nothing but one large silent protest. And in some ways, not so silent. It stirs rebellion and sedition and is a terrible chore for me to have to watch over every year. Especially when I have the Parthians to deal with on a regular basis. This country is an endless hole that swallows troops and treasure."

"Why doesn't Rome just put an end to this festival?"

"They don't have the troops to spare, and there is no public support for destroying a religious festival that no one has ever heard about. It can be a very reliable profit center. The temple can make us a lot of money. And it makes the barbarians happy. But not when they act like this. When they start acting like this, revenues go down and costs go up. I have to divert more troops and supplies. It's a terrible pain."

"How does the temple make Rome money? Taxes?"

"Partially. But here is the ingenious part. According to their god, they have to offer an animal sacrifice: a lamb. Most Jews can't afford to bring a lamb to the temple. And some of them are so far away that the lamb wouldn't be a lamb by the time it got here, it would be a sheep. So, when they get to the temple, they buy a lamb from the priests. But, according to their Jewish Laws, they cannot use Roman money to buy it."

"Why?"

"It is blasphemy. So, before they get to the temple, they have to exchange their Roman money for temple money. That way we hit the temple three times. The exchange fee, the purchase fee, and the taxes on the temple itself."

"How much do they pay?" Iovius asked.

"They pay Rome a tenth of their yearly earnings. But they also have to pay the temple for their god. So, it's altogether about one third. But they get their borders protected, they get to worship, and they don't have to volunteer into the legion."

"They don't have to fight?"

"No, they refuse to do anything on every seventh day. You can't have soldiers that refuse to march every seventh day."

"That's fortunate for them. But if you make so much money, why can't you fix the roads?"

"I only have a small budget allocated for road upkeep. Any roads I maintain will be torn up by the Parthians anyway. Most of the proceeds go back to Rome. That's the problem. They send me out here to administer this place and I have to place short term profit over long term investment and sustainability. They won't even let me raise swords against them."

"Why don't they erect more temples for their god. Closer to some big ports, get more foot traffic."

"They aren't allowed. One temple, one god," Pilate said.

"That's very simplistic, isn't it?"

Pilate stood up and let the cool water flow off him. He stepped out of the pool and entered the tepidarium, a medium-heated room. There he lay face down on a small wooden table and groaned. His golden-haired slave girl came up to him and poured olive oil all over his back from a terracotta pitcher. She spread the heated oil over his back and legs and began to give him a massage.

The arched ceiling was covered in stucco and a fine vapor. The floors were decorated with mosaics of nude nymphs and goddesses but the mosaics were missing several tiles and the floor was covered with dirt and grime from oil mixed with sweat.

Iovius followed Pilate into the small room, which was warmer than the frigidarium because it had one wall that was heated. He moved slowly and carefully as he didn't want to appear too comfortable in the governor's bath or be too familiar in general. He hoped Pilate would be more generous in business matters if the bath was received as a rare luxury.

Iovius had to stand because there was no room for another table in the tepidarium. As they spoke, he dripped the oil over himself. He stood by a bronze brazier which was heated from the furnace. The heat made his pores open and the oil felt more soothing.

"I can have someone do that for you?" Pilate said. He flipped over and closed his eyes as his young slave spread more oil from the heated pitcher over his body.

"No, that is alright. I think it would be too crowded." Iovius knew how particular people could be with their slaves, especially if they had golden hair. He didn't want Pilate to get upset.

"I insist, Iovius," Pilate said. He pulled on his slave's arm and pointed to Iovius. She set down her pitcher and walked over to Iovius.

The slave girl took the pitcher from him. She poured the oil over his body and began to rub it into his skin. Iovius saw Pilate look at him. He knew the only reason he had offered his slave to him was because he was interested in his business idea. Though Iovius knew he had Pilate's interest, he didn't want to ruin his advantage by seeming to enjoy Pilate's slave too much.

The governor just couldn't stop looking at her golden hair. The young slave girl had white skin and a healthy, plump body. Pilate made her wear her hair out and long.

"Where did you get a golden-haired one?" Iovius asked.

"From Gaul. I paid a fortune for her and another girl. The other one's hair turned brown but this one is as gold as the sun."

"She is beautiful. I am so jealous that you have one." Iovius thought complimenting Pilate might keep him calm and receptive.

"Tell me more about your business plan," Pilate said. "You were going to have empty ships transport cargo away from Rome."

"If I were a shipowner, I would offer low prices to transport things away from Rome, because if not, it's an empty trip and I get nothing. So, I have set up along this trade route to Egypt a shipping line that goes the other way. To take goods from Rome and import them into Ephesus, then take goods from Ephesus and export them to Myra, then take goods from there to Caesarea. We sell to buyers off the ports and pick up cargo.

"At these ports, there is always left-over cargo. They are exports that didn't sell or won't sell, or won't fit on the carts to the city. Or they are too old and might spoil. Most of the time they are packed back up and returned. This costs traders and ship commanders a lot of money. But because I would have transports going the other way, I could purchase those items for a large discount. They practically give this stuff away rather than have to cart it back.

"The prices will be less expensive because the transport costs are so low. When you add the discounted prices of the goods and the transportation, you get an inventory that you can unload at the next port for an extremely high profit."

After he was covered in oil, Pilate stood up and picked up a large leather ball that was twice the size of his head. It was heavy and he began tossing it up in the air to himself. Then Iovius stood across from him and they began passing the ball back and forth to each other. The exercise was designed to build up a sweat and clean the dirt from their pores.

"How do you expect to facilitate such a large operation at different ports?" Pilate asked.

"I have four sons, two brothers, and many cousins. We all have experience in trade and ship transportation."

"Is that right?"

"I have relationships with five ports so far. I can use the roads from Caesarea to the port and my shipments can arrive in Osti."

As they tossed the ball, Pilate stretched out his arms and neck. The sweat and the dirt mixed with oil to form a dark, dirty film over his entire body.

Pilate caught the ball and dropped it on the ground. He pointed at his slave woman who came over to him with a stringilis. Pilate sat on a marble bench while she took the large metal hook and scraped off the dirt that had mixed with the oil. The black waste was shaken off the stringilis and flung on the floor and walls.

Iovius took a stringilis and began to scrape the oil off his own body.

Once all the dirt and oil had been scraped off, the slave girl took a sponge and wiped Pilate's smooth white skin. She gave him a quick once over and plucked the few remaining hairs from his body as it was considered ugly in Roman society. He stood up and walked into the next room, the caldarium. Iovius quickly sponged himself off and followed. There was no time for him to pluck.

Before they stepped into the caldarium they put on elevated wooden sandals so the marble floor wouldn't burn their feet. The room was heated by the sun as well as a furnace that piped hot air through the walls and floor.

Pilate walked to the back of the square-shaped room and stepped into a sloped pool. Pilate reclined and let the heat move all over him, spreading over his legs and arms. The pool was too small for Iovius to get in as Pilate took up so much room. Instead he dipped his feet in and stretched out his neck. Nearby there was a round basin filled with cold water. Iovius took a small cup and drizzled some water over his head to cool himself down.

"Perhaps I shall go and make a sacrifice in their temple. Best to be in good standings with the local gods," Iovious said.

"You would not be permitted in the temple. You could only go into the outer court."

"Not permitted?"

"By penalty of death," Pilate added.

"I'm a Roman citizen, they can't sentence me to death."

"Yes, they can, they have authority to punish anyone who enters the temple. It was a consideration Rome gave the Jews for some reason," Pilate said. "They can administer their own justice."

"How many courts are there?" Iovius asked.

"Outer court, women's court, Israel court, and priest's court"

"A woman would be allowed to enter further than a Roman citizen! Who do they think they are? They can't keep me out."

"Don't. If you go into the temple, then the Jews will get upset and begin barking and howling and causing trouble. I'm having enough trouble with them at the moment. Just let me get through this stupid festival without incident. There is nothing to see anyway."

"No, I am a Roman citizen, this is a Roman city. I demand to be able to go in."

"Roman province, Iovius. No one cares. You didn't care until this very moment."

"Why does Rome allow these barbarians to act this way?"

"Two Jewish brothers, commoners, led a revolt against the Parthian governor in one of the border cities. These two barbarians became governors but were eventually murdered or removed or both. From time to time the Jews provide upheaval against the Parthian cities. This is very agreeable for us.

"The emperor wants to place a barbarian named Mithridates on the throne. They are having it out with Artabanus the second, or the third. Who can keep track of theses barbarian mongrels? But the emperor gives them a great deal of latitude so they can continue their insurgency against the Parthian border cities."

"What a horrible place," Iovius said hatefully. "They are smelly little creatures, aren't they?"

"Yes. They are barbarians, what do you expect?"

"Are there no bathing facilities here?"

"No, there is one in Caesarea. No, wait, they have baths. The high priest has a few of them, I hear. But it's not for bathing, it's for spiritual purity. It's just for ritual purposes."

"How do the people wash?" Iovius asked.

"In the river like animals. They have no desire to bathe like people of quality. For them, it is more of a spiritual bathing," Pilate said.

"Spiritual bathing?"

"Yes, it has a funny name as well. Hardalo! What is the priest bath called?"

Hardalo entered from outside the bath and bowed.

"Yes, sir?" Hardalo asked.

"What is the priest bath called, the spiritual bath?"

"A mikveh, sir."

Pilate and Iovius laughed hysterically. Pilate waved his arm for Hardalo to leave.

SECUNDUM MULTITUDINEM

Hardalo remained in the caldarium but kept his head bowed. "Sir, the commander needs to speak with you."

"What?" Pilate said, slightly irritated.

"More barbarians have gathered outside, sir," Hardalo said.

"More? What are they doing?" Pilate asked.

"They are sitting silently on the ground."

"Is that right? Animals. Send the commander in," Pilate said. Hardalo bowed and left.

Pilate quickly used a soft cloth to wipe the hot water away and then slowly got dressed.

"Commander," Pilate screamed. "Did you get more troops?" The commander entered and saluted.

"Yes, sir. I was able to get a translator to overhear a conversation between the high priest and Boaz. It was as you suspected; Boaz is agitating them over the standards."

"They were agitated over the standards all by themselves, Boaz was able to focus it. What else did the translator hear? Was he able to hear where Boaz and Herod found within themselves the impudence to challenge me?"

"The translator says that Boaz wants to force you to incite violence against the people so he may have you removed as governor."

"Is that right?" Pilate snapped. The commander remained silent. Pilate whipped his toga over his body. "Well, let's see if the crowd has that same conviction. I want you to station your troops around the mob. When I give the signal, I want the troops to draw their swords and start swinging them around. Have them yell and howl. I want these barbarians scared. But under no circumstances are they to cut anyone down. No blood. I want a show of force. We can't afford another suppression. Let's just see how committed these barbarian peasants are. Let's see if they are willing to die for King Herod and his advisors. Make sure they have a way to retreat out of the courtyard when you do this."

"Yes, sir," the commander said. He ran ahead to gather troops.

"When I commanded troops in Gaul, I always let them escape," Pilate said to Iovius.

Pilate stormed out onto the hot balcony and was stunned by the growing number of men in the courtyard. They were all bearded men with rough faces and backs weak from hard labor. Pilate tried not to breathe in the smell of their gross bodies and bad breath.

Boaz was in the center of the mob, holding his hands up and speaking a proclamation. Pilate instantly screamed over him.

"Very well, you barbarian mongrels. I have an offer for you. I will keep the standards where they are, and you will all disperse, or I will have you cut down like stocks of wheat."

He gave a signal with his arm and the commander encircled the crowd with soldiers three men deep. The Jewish crowd was still seated. As they looked up it seemed as though they were in a whirlpool of leather and iron.

"Now. Tell them to disperse," Pilate said to Boaz.

The translator spoke.

Boaz grabbed the collar of his tunic and pulled it to reveal his neck. He spoke roughly.

"He says they would rather be killed than suffer this blasphemy," the translator said.

"That's a deadly gamble. Are you sure you want to place that wager?" Pilate looked out and saw the Jews were all baring their necks in protest. Pilate lifted his hand again.

The commander and the soldiers took out their swords. The sound of metal blades being unsheathed amplified and reverberated from the walls. It sounded like packs of wild animals hissing. The soldiers barked and howled, swinging their swords and lunging at the mob.

Pilate stared at Boaz, waiting for the men around him to concede and run from the courtyard in terror.

Boaz spoke to Pilate in Latin. "Imagine what Rome will say about another Jewish massacre under your administration. It won't speak too well of your ability to maintain the peace. Word of this will only give evidence to your reputation, sir. You'll be recalled in an instant to Rome to stand trial for your mismanagement."

Pilate, enraged, lifted his hand to order his men to kill them all. Boaz smiled at him. If Pilate dropped his hand, all the Jewish men in the courtyard would be killed. But he knew Boaz was correct. He had already been warned. Killing these Jews during their holy festival would spark riot and revolt. He would be recalled to Rome and be forced to commit suicide to save the honor of the family name.

Pilate continued to stare at Boaz. They both knew that Pilate had been outmaneuvered. Boaz and his barbarian mob had called his bluff.

No one in the crowd moved. With one last glare at his opponent in the crowd, Pilate spun on his heels and retreated inside the Praetorium. Iovius followed, leaving the commander to get his troops to stand down without violence.

"Commander!" Pilate yelled as he marched down the open corridor. "I want you to wait until that barbarian dog is alone. Then I want you to arrest him and put him away somewhere. I want you to beat him. Whip him. I want to see the whites of his bones. Do you understand?" Pilate said. "I want his mob of followers to see him in such a state that they weep in terror."

"Yes, sir." The Commander saluted and ran off.

Pilate thought for a moment and realized how unwise it would be to damage the emissary of Herod. If Boaz was harmed, especially in a public setting, there would be a riot. Any confrontation with Boaz would cause a riot and a slaughter and eventually, his own suicide. "Commander!"

The Commander stopped and turned.

"Don't hurt him around his mob. That will cause a riot," Pilate said. "Just get him off the streets."

"Yes, sir."

The commander ran to the doorway to see if Boaz had moved. When he saw that he hadn't, he returned to Pilate.

"Boaz is still sitting in the courtyard with the mob. Do you want me to arrest him?"

"I want you to slit his throat so all those beggars can see," Pilate said in a spitting fury.

The commander hesitated for a moment. He slowly saluted and backed away.

"Commander," Pilate said. "No. Just watch him. Let me know if he leaves." He sighed in resignation. "Remove the standards from the streets. If anyone touches the soldiers, cut them down. Remove them as quickly and quietly as you can."

The commander saluted and left, more confident in his brief.

If I do nothing, I will appear weak and incompetent, Pilate thought. But, if I bring the soldiers down on them, I will appear disruptive, violent, and incompetent. Each choice will make a strong case to Rome that I should be replaced by King Herod Antipas, a local ruler who can manage them better – a barbarian king that would be able to rule them without disrupting the tax collections. It is a great stratagem, Pilate reluctantly admitted to himself.

Wait, Pilate thought. The high priest wasn't there, was he? No show of support from the priestly class. Perhaps there is dissension in the ranks that can be exploited. Maybe there is an opportunity to salvage the situation.

I need an agent, Pilate thought. Someone I can trust and who is unknown. He turned and saw Iovius standing quietly against the wall. Pilate held out his hand, motioning towards him.

"Iovius, you will perform an errand for me," Pilate said, taking Iovius by the arm.

"What errand?" Iovius said cautiously.

"As you can see, this is an exceedingly difficult place to keep orderly. Nobody in this city gets along and the population stirs at the strangest provocations."

"Yes, it appears very volatile here."

"And the orchestrator of these agitations is Boaz. But it isn't even him. It's Herod, the barbarian king. That barbarian has been able to buy more support than me. He's been collecting taxes off the peace I provide and buying support in Rome. Rome doesn't know what it is like. These people are not like other barbarians we've conquered in the past. They are unruly. It is impossible to fully conquer a people with an invisible god."

"You keep saying that. What does that mean?"

"Their god has no face or form. There is no representation or embodiment of him. He has no body. If you were to go into their temple, you wouldn't see this god. There are no statues or mosaics. They are not permitted to depict their god in any form. They aren't permitted to depict any human form. That is why they are so hostile to the standards. Their god doesn't live in the temple, he lives everywhere and nowhere. Do you see?"

"What's this errand?" Iovius asked.

"You will go to the high priest Caiaphas. He will tell you where to find Boaz's wife and children. You will then kill his wife and bring his children back here. I want his child next to me when I appear on the balcony again. I want to see the look on Boaz's face when he sees I'm holding the hand of his son."

"Kill his wife? I've never killed anyone. I'm a merchant."

"You are a Roman in the equites equo publico order. It is your duty to serve Rome."

"How do you expect me to do that?" Iovius asked.

"Take that knife attached to your belt and put the tip of it into his wife's neck all the way up to the hilt. Hail Caesar."

Iovius grabbed his knife. "This is a ceremonial dagger. It can't cut bread. Why don't you send one of your men?"

"They know what my men look like. You just arrived, no one knows who you are."

"But I'm obviously a Roman. I think they'll know I'm not there to worship their invisible god."

"Hardalo!" Pilate yelled and then turned back to Iovius. "They'll never suspect you. You're a merchant. And, you're half Greek, remember?" Hardalo entered and bowed. "Bring Iovius a dagger, a sharp one," Pilate told Hardalo, who bowed and rushed to another room.

"I can't do this."

"If you don't, I'll have you crucified."

"You can't crucify me, I'm a Roman citizen."

"If you fail to live up to your duties as an equites, I'll hammer in the nails myself. Don't come back here unless you finish your job," Pilate said with a coldness that made Iovius fear for his life. "Take the translator with you. Just in case that barbarian high priest wants to pretend that he can't speak your language. And make sure he knows how serious I am. You make sure he knows that if my post is taken from me and I'm recalled to Rome, the last order I give will be to burn this entire city to the ground and crucify every Jew in it."

Iovius had never considered the idea that he could be crucified. He remembered the horrible sight of the men outside the city gates, moaning and gurgling. He would do anything to keep from being crucified.

Hardalo returned with a shiny dagger in his hand. Pilate motioned and Hardalo forced it into Iovius' hands. It was heavy and cold, nothing like his ceremonial dagger.

ATRIUM SUMMI SACERDOS

Iovius was led through the city by the translator. The streets were crowded, and men were yelling and waving their hands. They passed one of the standards Pilate's troops had placed along the pathway. Jews were yelling and pushing each other in protest of the graven images. Troops had been dispatched by Pilate to remove the standards and five Roman soldiers were in the process of taking it down. The few troops were not able to work with any speed or skill because they had drawn their swords and gripped them tightly. They knew they could be easily overrun by the mob of angry Jews. They worked with one hand, while they held their swords tightly in the other. Iovius could see the rage and indignation on the Jewish people's faces. They hated the standards of Caesar so much that it seemed to cause them actual physical pain.

The translator, who was still dressed in peasant robes, rushed Iovius down a side street to avoid the standards. They walked towards the center of the city where there was a large fortified residence mounted on a hill.

"This is madness," Iovius said to the translator.

"There are no standards this way, sir. They won't be able to get you on this route," the translator said.

"I can't do this. I can't do this," Iovius said.

The translator had been told what Iovius was meant to do. His job was to make sure it was done and to report back any cowardice. If the merchant tried to run, the translator was ordered to kill him. If anything went wrong, the translator would be killed as well.

"I can't kill a woman. Or anyone. I've never killed anyone. Have you killed anyone?"

"Not like that."

"You do it," Iovius said in a panic.

"Me?"

"Yes, you do it."

"I can't."

"I'll pay you. Whatever you want, I'll pay you."

"I'd never get into the same building as Boaz's wife. They wouldn't let me past the front gates."

"You can take my clothes," Iovius said. "You can take my toga and gold ring. You will be dressed as an eques."

The translator played the idea through his mind. With the clothing and ring of the equites, I could travel to another city, he thought. I would be accepted into Roman life. I would have the seal and wax to a new life.

It was too much to hope for. He would have to kill Iovius. He wouldn't get halfway to the next town before he was hunted, captured, and brought back to Jerusalem to be crucified. The thought of being crucified sent a chill down his neck all the way to the stone ground. He would rather be killed by Boaz's guards for an assassination attempt than be crucified.

"I can't do it for you. You have to do it."

The translator led Iovius to the main entrance of the high priest's palace. It was a walled compound with arched wooden doors. The translator made his introductions to the guard at the door, who made Iovius surrender his ceremonial dagger before showing them inside. Iovius was surprised the guard didn't search him and discover the concealed one he was carrying. The guard was clearly reluctant to search a Roman of any position, let alone an eques.

The palace of the high priest contained arches made from stone. There were long open hallways and courtyards. It was grand and well-fortified with temple guards positioned aggressively around the walls. Iovius thought the entire residence was suspiciously luxurious for a temple priest in a backwater city no one had ever heard of.

Iovius was taken to a special chamber in the compound. It was a free-standing room that was not connected to the rest of the palace as non-Jews were not permitted inside the area reserved for priests. It appeared as if there were two rooms with a split down the middle. The separation allowed the high priest to receive visitors without breaking tradition and religious law.

Usually Iovius would have been indignant to be led into a special chamber. A Roman citizen deserved to be received in the main rooms of the palace. However, he was too busy being frightened to be indignant. The knife he kept under his tunic was weighing on his mind and wearing a blister into his hip.

"Hail Caesar," Caiaphas said as he entered the room.

Iovius was surprised to see a barbarian greet him in a Roman way. The priest is probably worried I will report any lapses in propriety to Pilate, he thought. "Hail Caesar," Iovius replied.

Iovius was rattled. He knew that he was frightened and would appear weak if he allowed the high priest to see it. He took a deep breath to compose himself. This is just another port negotiation, he thought to himself. Just another negotiation.

"I'm impressed you speak Latin. I thought we were going to have to struggle through a translator." He opened his negotiation with a slight insult. Let's see how he deals with that, he thought.

"My guards tell me you are an emissary from Pilate. How may I assist our honorable governor?" Caiaphas ignored the Roman's taunt. He had become far too accustomed to them.

"I'm not going to lie to you; he's not happy."

"No, I would expect not."

"And, if you don't mind me saying so, you don't look very happy."

"My happiness is meaningless; I only serve God."

"Right." Iovius was dismissive of Caiaphius' piousness, he was preoccupied with trying to figure out how to get the location of his future murder victim. "Look, what's your name?"

"I am the high priest, Joseph, son of Caiaphas."

"Right." The name was so foreign to Iovius that he immediately forgot it. "High priest, why do you think I'm here?"

"I believe that Pilate has sent you here to appeal to the people to keep the standards from being removed."

"No, he has already ordered the standards to be removed."

Caiaphas' eyes opened wide.

"Yes, you can imagine how angry that made him."

"Does he blame me for that?" Caiaphas asked.

"Like I said, he's not happy. But he's mostly not happy with someone else. Can you imagine who that is?"

Caiaphas tried to mask his panic and fear.

"If he were going to create a ranking of who was going to be crucified, it would be Boaz at the top, followed by you as a close second, and me and every other Jew in this city as tied for third. Look, you seem like a practical man. A businessman even. We have to find a way to deal with this situation before it gets out of hand."

"What does the governor want from me?"

"He wants Boaz's wife and children."

Caiaphas closed his eyes in discomfort. He knew that Pilate was a brutal and methodical man. The escalation he had tried to warn Boaz of had begun. His mind began to scramble. How can I contain this, he thought? Pilate won't stop at Boaz and his family.

"Boaz's wife and children are guests of King Herod Antipas. They are staying at his palace. The palace is well fortified and guarded."

Iovius sighed in relief. With the wife and children safe in Herod's palace, he would not be able to accomplish his mission. He wouldn't have to carry out his charge after all. His relief, however, was replaced by dread when he realized he would have to explain to Pilate that his plan to murder the wife and kidnap the children was impossible.

"What do we do, high priest?" Iovius asked desperately. "I think you know why he sent me and what he sent me for. This doesn't end it. It just makes the governor more desperate."

"Is he desperate?" Caiaphas asked.

"I think he already has crosses picked out for us." Iovius could see the panic in the high priest's eyes. "What do we do?"

"The governor must know, I'm not the one sending reports of him to his superiors. That is Herod Antipas."

"That would be hard to convince him of, considering you were standing next to him outside his palace a few hours ago."

"It was only to keep up appearances. I would lose all credibility with the people if I hadn't. I can't be seen to go against Boaz by the people. Herod and the people would accuse me of being a Roman collaborator. How can I serve the governor if I am seen to ignore our most sacred traditions? I've never missed a payment to him from the temple."

"If I were you, I would start thinking about how you can serve the governor. And soon. He told me his last official act, if he is forced out of his post, would be to burn the city to the ground."

"There is nothing I can do," Caiaphas said.

"I disagree. I can think of something. I see you have guards all around you here."

"My temple guards?"

"Yes, very impressive. You need to use them. If I were you, I would find a way to compel Boaz to be less unruly. Or find a way to calm the people of the city. If you want your temple to remain upright, I would find a way to keep the trouble makers off the streets."

NOLITE INTERFICERE NUNTIUS

It was a long walk back to the governor's palace. Iovius had no idea what he was going to say to him. He walked as slowly as he could to prolong the confrontation without putting himself at risk of being uncovered as a Roman on the streets of a highly volatile city. He could not dismiss the overwhelming paranoia that these foreigners knew he was on the streets to kill one of their leader's family.

Pilate was reviewing the tax collections for the day with his advisor. He was fidgeting and having trouble concentrating on the figures. He had to divert troops from the outskirts of the city to help defuse a tense situation regarding the standards. He was already short-handed from having to send away a cohort to defend the border against the Parthians. Fewer troops would make it more difficult to police the city during the festival without the added tension of this standard nonsense. His mind wandered to Iovius and the mission he had been charged with.

"The totals are in for today," Hardalo said.

"Did we make our quota?"

"No, sir."

"How much money did we lose?" Pilate asked.

"We are around one quarter in deficit from our estimated goal."

Pilate was so angry he kicked the wooden table, sending a sharp pain through his shin. "Why is it so low?" Pilate demanded.

"There was a disturbance at the exchange tables today."

"A disturbance put us down one quarter?"

"It almost caused a riot," Hardalo said cautiously.

"Do you think we'll be able to make it up?"

"Maybe, if there is no more trouble. At all. And even then, I'm not sure."

Pilate took an oil jug and threw it against the wall. The small jug didn't shatter, so he walked over, picked up the jug, and threw it again. It broke into shards and dust. Pilate knew that the only way of explaining the short tax revenue would be to show the increased amount of unrest with the local Jewish population. He would explain one failure by admitting another.

"Do I have the credit to borrow to make up the deficit?"

"There is no lender, no ten lenders that would have the funds to make up the deficit."

"I want you to bring the high priest here. I want him to give me some sacred treasure from the temple. What do they call that, the treasure?"

"They call it corban, sir."

"Yes, I want the high priest to offer me corban to help pay for the taxes that are to be sent back to Rome. Do we know how much they have?"

"They don't give us exact figures. Last time you spoke to the high priest he said the majority had already been used to build the aqueduct."

"Have him offer the remainder. That should help." Pilate knew he was running out of options. "We could borrow from the publicani," he blurted out. "What rate does he charge?"

"Ten percent per month."

"Ten percent! That's outrageous!"

The translator entered and bowed to Pilate. "Sir, Iovius of the Domitius, equites equo publico has returned."

"I don't see a little barbarian boy behind you," Pilate said, keeping his furious eyes trained on his daily tax figures.

"The wife and children are being held at King Herod's palace. It would be impossible for me to get to them," Iovius said, his voice weak. He was nauseous and dizzy with fear and dread.

Pilate's face flushed and became hot. He grabbed the back of Iovius' neck and punched him in the stomach. Iovius coughed and fell to his knees. Pilate brought a dagger from under his tunic and put it to Iovius' throat.

"Don't worry. This one isn't ceremonial."

Iovius was certain Pilate was about to kill him. At least he wouldn't have to endure crucifixion. He looked into the governor's eyes and saw a blank stare. It was as though Pilate was dismissing reasons, one after the other, as to why Iovius shouldn't be killed.

There was only one thing that saved Iovius. It was a thought that had helped Pilate show restraint in the face of danger to get his military and political posts. It was a thought that served him in all his dealings with politicians and barbarians. He thought, what if I need him later?

Pilate let him go and put his knife away. Iovius coughed and gagged.

"You look tired, Iovius," Pilate said. "Shall we have a bath?"

During the bath, Pilate was distant and silent. He didn't speak to Iovius or make any sound at all. He stared off towards the wall. He was deep in thought or frightened, perhaps.

"You mustn't be angry with me, Iovius," Pilate said. "You can see the stress I'm under here."

"The strain must be unbearable." Iovius was still frightened but he knew he had to ignore the attempt on his life. He tried to keep from trembling.

"Tell me more about this business idea you have."

"There is little more to tell. We buy goods that don't fit on the boats going to Rome for a large discount and ship them the other way."

"Yes, but what do you have in the way of materials. What do you need to start the business?"

"I would need permission from the local governments and a few patrons to get the operation started with funding," Iovius said. He was not as enthusiastic about enlisting the help of Pilate since he was almost murdered by him.

"And what would you need from me?" Pilate asked.

"A letter of introduction would be most appreciated. Perhaps you could introduce me to some patrons or families of quality."

"What would my percentage be?"

Iovius was rattled. He didn't expect Pilate to be so interested or so bold in his interest. "I don't know if you would want to be a part of something so pedestrian. Besides, I wouldn't want to impose on our friendship."

"Nonsense. Nothing strengthens a bond of friendship like a strong shipping business. I can give you your introductions and help with some materials. For this, I will take fifty percent. Fifty percent of the total revenue."

"Fifty percent? That percentage of revenue doesn't leave very much for me to pay for the operations." Iovius was rattled. He was negotiating percentages with a man who had held a knife to his throat just a few moments ago.

"How much would you need?"

"For the first year or so, I would need all of it."

"All of it? Is that right? Okay. Perhaps it would be better if you paid me a patronage fee upfront and then I'll only take thirty percent."

"I don't know if I can afford that," Iovius said. "I'll have to run some figures and speak with my cousin before I can be sure what an affordable number would be." Iovius was hoping to stall the negotiations. He didn't want Pilate to be so heavily involved in the business. He also didn't want Pilate to take all the money before the business was even operating. If I can just stall him for a couple of days, he thought, I'll be able to leave the city and try another avenue.

PONTIFEX OSTIUM

Pilate and Iovius were drinking wine in the bath. The yellow firelight danced off the walls. Hardalo entered and bowed.

"Excuse me, sir. Caiaphas, the high priest, respectfully wishes permission to speak with you."

"I didn't mean I wanted to talk about the temple treasure during my bath." Pilate laughed.

"I didn't send for him. He came on his own."

"At this hour?" Pilate asked. "Shouldn't he be howling at the moon or whatever these barbarians do at night?"

"He said it was a matter of the utmost importance, sir."

"Is that right? Well, send him in," Pilate said.

"He said he can't enter a non-Jewish building; it will defile him. He respectfully asks if you would grant him an audience outside."

"Oh, does he? Does he indeed?" Pilate splashed the wine from his cup violently onto the floor. "Well, you just tell him if he wants to see me, he can come in here or he can shove off."

"Yes, sir." Hardalo bowed and walked towards the door.

"Demanding little buggers, aren't they?" Pilate said, taking a drink. "At night?" Pilate said to himself, thinking out loud. "He doesn't want anyone to see him." Pilate yelled out, "Hardalo?"

"Yes, sir," Hardalo said, trotting back.

"Hardalo, did he come to the south entrance?"

"Yes, sir."

"Are the barbarians still outside?" Pilate asked. "At the north entrance?"

"The crowd has thinned out a small amount."

"Is Boaz still there?"

"Yes, sir."

Pilate raised his hand, calculating imaginary figures. "I think I will see him."

"Yes, sir."

"Is there a problem?" Iovius asked. "Would you like me to go?"

"An opportunity. No, stay, we have a lot to discuss still."

Pilate walked along the cool tiled floor carrying a small lamp. He muttered to himself, rehearsing what he was going to say. He had made the attendant run ahead of him to make sure the guards were out of sight.

Caiaphas was pacing outside the south entrance. He was keeping to the shadows, making sure no one could see him. The temple guards that had been watching over him had silently vanished. He became frozen and immediately apprehensive.

Pilate appeared from a long corridor that led to the entranceway like a ghost. Caiaphas saw him, bowed courteously, and began to walk to him. Pilate was still and arresting.

"Governor." Caiaphas stopped when he saw that in order to be close to Pilate, he would have to enter the structure. Aside from the Jewish law which forbade him to enter, the frescos of naked women, graven images, and depictions of other Roman gods offended him.

"With your permission, I would like to speak with you about something." He had to project his voice to be heard. The sound echoed off the offensive frescos and tiles. The hallway was a large gulf, it was impossible to be heard without shouting or to maintain any comfortable privacy. Caiaphas struggled to speak softly.

"Please, what's on your mind?" Pilate asked, setting his lamp on a mantel beside him.

"As you know, governor, this is a delicate time. And people, at such times, are easily confused—"

"I'm sorry, I can't hear you. You'll have to speak louder," Pilate said.

"Sir, people at this time are easily confused. And some take it upon themselves to spread their blasphemies to the common people. There is one, in particular, who sees it fit to damn the souls of his neighbors—"

"I still can't hear you," Pilate said, interrupting.

"With your permission, sir, if you could come closer—"

"Do not give me an order, animal!" Pilate shouted. His voice distorted as it echoed off the walls.

"No, sir, I wouldn't dare—"

"If I didn't know better, I would say you were embarrassed to be known to meet with me this evening."

"No, sir, I am not permitted—"

"Or perhaps you believe I am your servant, to be summoned from an evening's bath to your bidding? Is that right? No, you stand there because I allow it. You serve me because I allow it. I will not have my position compromised by a barbarian mongrel who thinks he can outmaneuver me with rumors and correspondence flung at my superiors. And if for one instant I think you are trying to compromise my service to Rome, I will have you removed and crucified. Hail Caesar!"

Caiaphas was still with fear as he looked across the hallway and saw the distant figure smooth out his robe.

"Hail Caesar," Caiaphas said meekly in resignation.

Pilate held out his hand, motioning for the high priest to cross the courtyard. Caiaphas reluctantly stepped over the threshold and walked towards Pilate. He could see in the dim lamplight the frescos of naked nymphs seducing men by ponds and regal engravings of the foreign emperor. He was humiliated and shamed. Each step he took, he hated himself even more. This is to keep the temple standing, he told himself. This is to keep our traditions alive.

He reached Pilate. He had the posture of one who had just been beaten with a club.

"Now, what is your problem?" Pilate asked.

"There is a man who claims himself to be a messiah. He was caught—"

"Crucify him. Commander!" he called out. "Crucify him, find his confederates and his family and crucify them as well. Anything else?" he said briskly to Caiaphas.

"We have a member of his inner twelve who is willing to testify that he claims to be the messiah," Caiaphas offered.

"No need for a trial, we'll just crucify him with all the others in the morning. Wait, you haven't already had your barbarian trial?"

"No."

"Why don't you just put him to death? You don't need Rome for that."

"He claims to be a messiah."

"But after all the howling about keeping your traditions and wanting to police all local matters yourselves, this seems odd," Pilate said. "Especially on the night of the festival when you should be celebrating with your families. Very odd. Could you not convene your council for a trial? Or were you afraid to? A Roman trial by night in the dark is a much safer option for you, is that right? More private?"

"I knew Boaz was putting you in a hard situation. I wanted to show my support for you and help you manage the situation," Caiaphas said, scrambling for words.

"And it also allows you to get rid of a troublemaker at the same time. What thrift. It makes no difference to Rome. This messiah will meet the fate of all kings. Commander, take him into custody."

"Yes, sir," the commander said as he turned the corner.

"Thank you, sir. We will bring him at once." Caiaphas was eager for the night to be over.

"Bring him? You already have him?"

"Yes, sir."

"He must be very dangerous to you. Is that right?" Pilate asked with a mocking smile.

"No, sir. I wanted you to know we are loyal to Caesar. Herod and his representatives have been acting shamefully. We thought we could better serve Rome by acting swiftly."

"Swiftly. At night. When no one is watching. No trial. Perhaps your messiah is rallying the support of the people. Perhaps, your people wouldn't stand for his arrest. It can be such a nuisance when public opinion is twisted away from you. How embarrassing.

"We have him and a member of his 12, his inner circle. He is ready to bear witness as to this man's crimes—"

"Don't worry, I've already sentenced him to be crucified. Don't bother with the explanation, just crucify him."

"Yes, sir."

"Commander..." Pilate stopped and thought for a moment. His mind was jumping from idea to idea. Did I take the right path? he wondered. If I crucify a Jewish rebel, will all the followers fall into line? No, he thought, they will rally around Boaz. And Boaz will send them all to have their throats cut so Herod has a case to replace me. Wait, he thought, stopping immediately. Herod is the answer.

"Where do you have him?" Pilate asked as he approached Caiaphas.

"I have him under guard at my—"

"From the Galilee, is that right?" Pilate asked, stepping towards him. "You said this messiah is from the Galilee?"

"Yes, sir," Caiaphas said.

"Commander, take the prisoner to Herod. Ask him what is to be done with him."

"Herod?" the commander asked.

"Yes. That beggar wants to be king, let him be king. Bring him a messiah from his province that challenges his kingship. This rebel is from the Galilee. King Herod oversees law and order in the Galilee. This is his problem now. Rome isn't going to do all his hard work for him. Let's see how endearing he is to his people when he kills one, just as Rome would. And when Herod orders him to death, you make sure everyone knows it is Herod's orders. Take this rebel and make sure he tells everyone in front of his court. I want everyone to hear. You understand? Let's see how this barbarian really likes bearing the responsibility of law and order."

"Yes, sir," the commander said, though he was uncertain about the meaning of the request.

"And, commander. Take him through all the front doors. In front of everyone. Make a spectacle of it. Really dress it up for him. I want Boaz and the mob to see that you are taking this prisoner to Herod."

"Yes, sir."

"Perhaps I will look to our friends the Parthians. I'll fling arrows at them while they chase me. Excellent."

Pilate clapped his hands as he returned to the dining area and patted his merchant friend on the shoulder. "Do you see, Iovius? Resolved. I told you these barbarians didn't know who they were dealing with." Even though Pilate was putting on a show for those around him, the idea of having been outmaneuvered by a barbarian earlier in the day made the anger swell up in him.

Iovius clapped along with Pilate. "Very good," he said. "Very impressive." Iovius was more relieved than Pilate because he knew that if the governor had no way of claiming a victory, no one would be safe from his rage.

"We should eat," Pilate said. "I've had some of the more rustic cuisines. It's quite good, though a little robust for my taste. But the cooks have found a wonderful combination of local and proper Roman tastes."

Pilate led Iovius into the triclinium. The room was ornately decorated with mosaics on the floor and paintings on the walls and ceilings. There were three lectus triclinaris, or couches, arranged in the shape of a horseshoe, surrounding a low, square table.

Pilate and Iovius spread themselves out on the couches like lazy cats. Pilate's slave girl took his sandals and placed them in the corner.

Their heads were positioned towards the mensa, the low square table. Their left elbows propped on cushions and their feet on the outside of the dinner couch. The slave girl refilled their wine cups using a ladle. They dipped their hands in small bowls of water to wash off their fingers. There were two bowls with bread and nuts.

The slave girl returned and served the starters. On a large tray stood a bronze donkey. On its back were two baskets, one holding green olives, and the other black. On either side were dormice, dipped in honey and rolled in poppy seeds. Nearby, on a silver grill, lay small steaming sausages.

The first course was brought out on the mensa. Eggs boiled in wine with pine nuts and garum sauce.

"Have some eggs with your garum," Pilate said.

"You can never have enough garum," Iovius replied. The garum sauce was a fermented fish sauce used as a condiment.

The first table was taken away and a fresh bowl was brought out to dip their hands in. The slave girl brought out the second mensa with the second course, mensa secunda boiled goat with dipping sauces.

The slave-girl bent down and whispered into Pilate's ear.

"Is that right?" Pilate said. He turned to Iovius. "Apparently they have prepared some of the sauces with your spices."

"Oh good, you must tell me how fresh they are. I paid a large premium for seemingly above average quality."

"Do any of your slaves have any special entertainment skills?" Pilate asked.

"Oh yes, I have one woman who is a remarkable singer. She is from the desert so her songs are barbaric. But they are haunting. I shall send for her if you like."

"By all means. Hardalo!" Pilate screamed. Hardalo entered and bowed. "I need you to fetch one of Iovius' slaves."

"Her name is Clousta," Iovius said.

"Yes, sir." Hardalo bowed and left.

Iovius needed to change the subject to keep Pilate from flying into a rage again. He needed to steer the conversation to something that wouldn't remind the governor of the barbarians and Herod. "Is it true they mutilate the men's genitals?" Iovius asked. It was the only thing he could think of.

"Oh, yes, every one of them. It's fascinating. Hardalo!" Pilate called out in a shriek. Hardalo entered and bowed. "Have the guards bring us a Jewish prisoner. You seem to be fascinated with barbarian's genitals."

"Yes, sir," Hardalo said.

"Yes, I must confess it is a subject that fills me with great interest to which I'm certain I shall receive ridicule from you to no end. But there is something primordial about it. Truly remarkable," Pilate said.

Two guards entered with one of the many Jewish prisoners who were to be crucified in the morning. He was shaking and weak.

"Take off his clothes, we want to see his genitals," Pilate said.

The guards stripped the prisoner like he was peeling fruit.

"That is incredible," Iovius said, staring intently at the prisoner's penis. "Why do they do that?"

"It's part of the covenant with their god."

"Covenant? What is the covenant?"

"I think it has something to do with stone tablets."

"Stone tablets?"

"Yes, they need stone tables to keep the goats in place."

"What happens if the goats get out?"

"Oh, it upsets the Jewish god. That's why the genitals must be mutilated. To remind them to keep the goats behind the stone tablets."

The Jewish prisoner passed out from exhaustion and hunger and fell on the floor.

"That's amazing," Iovius said.

"Did it hurt?" Iovius asked the prisoner.

"He can't understand you," Pilate said. "He can't speak any civilized language." Pilate waved his hand and the guards removed the prisoner from the floor. "They came from Egypt to this wonderful land you find yourself in."

"They decided to settle a long way from civilization, didn't they?"

"On no, they didn't settle here. This land was given to them by their god."

"Given to them by their god? What have they done to offend this god?" Iovius laughed.

"Being industrious with a small fuel of curiosity, I took it upon myself to become educated in the ways of the Jews. They have a document that outlines the history of their god and people. I tried to have one of the priests read it to me. He refused. I found someone to translate for me and the entire text is a list of rules and laws and logistics that govern said laws. Two goats for every goat someone steals. No lifting of more than an acorn on Saturdays. It's maddening. Their god must be the dreariest of all taskmasters."

Hardalo returned with Clousta. She was a young woman with dark braided hair. Iovius took Clousta aside and whispered excitedly into her ear.

"You had better sing your heart out. He needs to be in a good mood, or we'll be in trouble."

"What should I sing?" she asked.

"A song good enough not to have our throats cut."

The slave was instantly terrified.

"Is there some problem?" Pilate asked.

"No, of course not, I just want her to understand the quality and rank of who she is performing for."

"Is that right?" Pilate said, slightly amused.

The woman began to sing. She fumbled over her trills and quickly lost her breath. She forgot her words and had to stop the song halfway through. She was so frightened and lowered her head.

"Come here, woman," Pilate said. He put his wine cup on the table. He began to touch her and inspect her. "Sturdy," he said to himself. "Bring in the drinks," he yelled out. With a cup in his hand, he turned towards Iovius. "Make her sing again."

REGEM IN ATRIUM

The commander collected the Jewish prisoner and led a small company of troops out through the courtyard. The troops barreled their way through the crowd forcing them to move aside. They were confused to see a Jewish man being pushed along at sword point. The troops weren't leading him to be crucified as he was being led in the opposite direction towards Herod's palace. The commander held a torch so Boaz and the crowd could easily track them.

When the commander reached the palace, he was shown immediately to a small anti-chamber. He could see Herod down a long hall lounging on pillows with his wife as he held court. Herod got up and walked around slowly, then made a large display of sitting back down. An advisor entered and bowed as he approached Herod's seat.

"Yes?" Herod said stifling a yawn. He waved at the advisor to move closer so he could speak more privately.

"Sir, there is someone here to see you. It is a Roman commander."

"Later, let him wait," Herod said.

"He's on an errand for the governor," the advisor said.

"Pilate's commander?" Herod looked away in concern. He stood up quickly, kicking pillows onto the ground. His wife was annoyed at the jarring commotion. "Did he appear hostile?"

"No, sir. He was most respectful."

"What does he want?"

"He said he is presenting a prisoner for judgment."

"For judgement?" Herod asked.

Herod swept his arm and the advisor bowed as they exited the banquet area.

The commander waited in the antechamber, leaning against a wall. He carefully studied the geometric designs decorating the room. The squares and rectangles seemed very barbaric and simple to him.

Herod entered with a wide sweep of his arms. His face was red from laughing and drinking. He saw the commander and gave him a condescending smile.

"Hail Caesar," Herod said with derision.

The commander bowed his head, he would be killed before he responded to this barbarian king as a Roman. Herod hid his fat belly behind a brightly-colored robe with golden geometric designs. He wore a large elaborate headdress and had a thick greying beard.

"Sir, I have come on behalf of Governor Pilate to deliver a prisoner for your judgement."

"A prisoner? From Pilate?"

"Yes, sir. A Jew."

"A Jew? It is my understanding that Jews are to be tried by the full Sanhedrin during the day. I was not aware that the Sanhedrin convened during the night of the festival."

"I don't know the nature of Jewish law."

"No, I expect not. What is the nature of his crime?"

"A messiah."

"It is that time of year, isn't it? Ah, in what circumstance did our wise governor see fit for me to judge this messiah?" Herod asked.

"I don't understand."

Herod held back a condescending sigh. "Why would he want my judgement on such an offense? There were dozens of prisoners that didn't require my judgement for this morning's crucifixions.

"As a matter of jurisdiction."

"Jurisdiction." Herod thought for a moment. "When, if you will grant me, did the governor come upon this decision?"

"When he heard the prisoner was from the Galilee."

Herod was grinning with amazement. He couldn't believe Pilate would defer to a barbarian. Herod immediately considered the

Roman saying, 'Beware the Greeks, even when they bring gifts.' This can only be a strategy of some kind, Herod thought.

"The governor said all that?"

"Yes."

Herod walked over to the wall and lifted a large thick curtain revealing a doorway to a hall that led to the main reception area. Down the hall, conversations could be heard in the courtyard by Herod's guests.

"I'm sorry, commander, my barbarian ears are very weak. Perhaps if you project your voice and I stand over here I will better be able to understand."

"Of course," the commander said. He was barely able to contain his rage at being ordered about by a barbarian. He knew Pilate wanted to make sure everyone heard so he had no choice but to comply.

"You are too gracious," Herod said.

The commander walked towards the door and stood with one foot outside in the hall.

"Governor Pilate has ordered me to remit this case of treason to his Kingship Herod," the commander said. Herod couldn't stop smiling. "May you pass judgement on this prisoner?

"I waive all jurisdiction and defer judgement to the governor in this matter," Herod said.

The commander was shocked. "What?"

"Yes, please give the governor my best." Herod snapped the curtain closed and turned towards the commander and spoke softer. "And please tell him that I am, of course, a dutiful servant of the governor and Rome."

"You don't want to pass judgement?" The commander begged, hoping Herod hadn't seen through Pilate's plan.

"No. No. No," Herod said casually. "I think the governor is better suited to this man. I can only imagine he has no choice but to execute him. Such is the burden of authority, I expect," Herod said mockingly. "Here, allow me to present the governor with this." Herod gave the commander a purple tunic he had worn over his shoulders. "A gift for our noble governor."

Herod returned to his pillows with a large self-satisfied grin.

The commander put his helmet back on and escorted the prisoner out of the palace. Herod watched through the window as the commander led the prisoner and five other soldiers out through the courtyard. He enjoyed the spectacle. That was very desperate of Pilate, Herod thought. Now he has cornered himself even more by making such a show of it. I'll be king sooner than I thought.

The commander slowly approached Pilate and Iovius. They were drinking wine and watching a young slave woman dance.

The commander hesitantly removed his helmet and leaned down next to Pilate.

"How did he receive it?" Pilate said. "Was he a good little boy? Did the barbarians hang the prisoner from his palace walls?" Pilate laughed, taking a large sip of wine. "How did he have him executed?"

"Sir. He deferred his judgement to you and returned the prisoner to your custody."

"What!" Pilate slammed his food back onto the table.

"He presented this to you as a gift." The commander gave Pilate the purple tunic. This was more than Pilate could bear. This was the final insult. A gift from the barbarian who spits in his face. Were Herod not so well patronized in Rome, Pilate would have slit his throat himself.

Pilate erupted into a violent rage. He began throwing food against the wall and kicking the serving tables. One of the water vases shattered, sending a small shard into his leg. He began to bleed.

Hardalo quickly cleaned the wound with water from a pitcher and dressed it with a cloth as Pilate continued to drink heavily. While Hardalo tied the grey cloth around his leg, Pilate looked at the others in the room. He noticed the slave girl cowering in the corner. The sight of blood and the violence had frightened her, and she was trying to hide. Pilate enjoyed seeing the girl frightened of him. A little blood can go a long way, he thought.

"Just crucify him tomorrow with the others early in the morning before the barbarians are awake," Pilate said.

"Yes, sir," the commander said.

MANE DILUCULO

Pilate awoke early in the morning with a hangover. His head ached and he limped from the gash in his leg. He had Hardalo clean it, apply ointment and a new bandage.

"Bring me a wet cloth for my head," he demanded.

When Hardalo returned he spread the cloth over his face. "And am I right in assuming that the crowds have dispersed?" Pilate leaned back and wrung the water from the cloth over his head.

"I will go check, sir," Hardalo said.

After a quick meal of nuts and bread, Pilate began his daily administration duties of reading over ledgers with his advisors. They sat cross-referencing different accounts of money and taxes.

"The temple has made another request to borrow funds to purchase the right to use more space in the garbage refuse," an advisor said.

"How much?"

Hardalo entered the room and quickly approached Pilate.

"How are the barbarians this morning?" Pilate asked.

"They say they are followers of a rabbi we have in custody."

"What is a rabbi again?"

"A priest."

"Is that right?" Pilate said.

"Yes, sir."

"I see," Pilate said, uninterested. "Tell them they can see him later outside the gates." He laughed to himself. Men were taken outside the gates to be crucified.

"They appear to have the makings of agitators. Worse than yesterday."

Pilate threw the cloth onto the floor and turned around. "Agitators!"

"Yes, sir. A few of them left in the night, but since dawn, more seem to have gathered. The translator said they are followers of one of the prisoners you have and are very upset."

"Which one?"

"I don't know, sir. I believe it is the one Caiaphas sent us. The one Herod refused to take into custody; from the Galilee."

Pilate became enraged. The commander entered to find Pilate screaming at his advisors.

"This is utter nonsense! I can't administrate this city if I can be undermined by a barbarian king with more money to buy support. It's Rome. They are to blame. They don't give me the tools to properly work in this wasteland." He turned to the commander. "Take all the men you can, kill every single one of those barbarian bastards," Pilate said, throwing his cup of water against the wall. "I want each one of them dead in a hole and covered in dirt by nightfall."

"Sir, perhaps you would like to discuss this situation with your advisors," the commander said.

"Kill them all! Each one, then hang the bodies from their feet!"

Hardalo stood silent while Pilate had his tantrum. Pilate kicked and stomped and spat. He knew that he had been outmaneuvered by a barbarian and he would be recalled to Rome and forced to commit suicide. This small barbarian city would be the ruin of his family name. All the work he had done on the battlefields in Gaul and the halls of the senate in Rome would be looked over because of these foreigners. People would speak his name as a joke.

"Hardalo," Pilate called out.

"Yes, sir."

"Go to the translator and find out which prisoner they are calling for."

"Yes, sir."

Hardalo bowed and ran down the hall, pleased to be away from the governor.

Pilate's leg was throbbing. He leaned over to examine the wound from last night by pulling the cloth away. The pinch caused him to gasp. The dried blood had attached to the wound and it was ripped open when he pulled the cloth away. The blood began to gush out again. He quickly attempted to apply the clean rag.

He remembered the slave girl from last night who had been disturbed by the blood. He remembered the military tactics from his wars in Gaul. A threat of harm or death is meaningless, Pilate thought. Any threat is meaningless unless they can see it. The barbarians need to see blood for them to be able to imagine it. A little imagination goes a long way when it comes to blood. I just need to show them a little blood.

Pilate walked towards the window and looked out. He smiled to himself as he thought. Suddenly, he realized something. "No, wait. Get the commander back in here."

"Hail Ceasar," the commander said.

"I want you to find this prisoner they are gathering outside for. Caiaphas's prisoner."

"Yes, sir."

"Don't execute him just yet. Make a spectacle of him, then bring him to the courtyard. Make it all look very dramatic. I want the very sight of him to turn Hades white. I want blood, I want bruises, and I want to see bone. Do you understand? Dress it up for them. Make sure his followers can recognize him, but barely. Do you understand? I want them to hear his screams. I want them to see how helpless they really are."

"Yes, sir."

"The only thing these barbarians understand is blood. So, I need to give them a demonstration of how Rome can draw blood. I want him humiliated. I want each and every barbarian to look at this rabbi and think, I will do anything to keep that from happening to me."

"Yes, sir."

"I need to change clothes. Bring me my armor," Pilate ordered. "I want them to see real might."

This was war and it was eminently appropriate that he dress for battle.

Pilate removed his white equestrian tunic and put on his red battle tunic. Hardalo laced up his armor from the back and draped the long cape over the metal. The armor was yellow gold and marble white. The chest plate was silver-colored with gold relief of a charioteer. The polished gold was almost blinding in the morning sun. He had a turquoise sash and a red cape wrapped around his arms and back. Dangling from his side he wore his golden dagger. It was not ceremonial.

He looked like a regal statue. A symbol of Rome's marshal might and opulent magnificence.

Hardalo escorted Iovius to Pilate. Iovius entered drinking a cup of wine. He hadn't been able to sleep for fear of Pilate becoming angry and having him killed, or possibly crucified. There were only a few more days left until Pilate left the city to return to his headquarters. Iovius only had to remain out of the way until then to stay alive.

"Come along, Iovius, I want you to watch this." Iovius was very worried about watching. If Pilate was humiliated or outmaneuvered again, Iovius would prefer not to bear witness to it.

ULTIMA COLLATIO

Pilate entered the balcony overlooking the small courtyard. As before, a crowd of Jews had gathered. Some of them had been a part of the protest to have the standards removed but many of the faces were new. Once Pilate was seen, an angry hush fell over the crowd.

Pilate was wearing better clothes and finery than most had ever seen. The deep colors and gold jewelry sparkled in the morning sun. He was flanked by soldiers, advisors, a translator, and Iovius. It was an intimidating assembly.

They were surprised to see Pilate in such dress. They hadn't expected the Roman to dress up for the occasion. When the crowd saw him, they felt as though their wind had been taken from them. Boaz stood up and presented himself. He knew this was an intimidation technique and a desperate one at that. He knew Pilate couldn't attack them, even if the governor dressed as the god of war.

"Good morning," Pilate said, opening his arms. The translator spoke to the crowd in Aramaic. The crowd was silent, squinting from the polished gold and silver. "Why have you assembled here?"

One of the men in the front of the crowd answered before Boaz could respond. The translator spoke.

"He says they have come for their rabbi," the translator said. Boaz couldn't believe his luck. He had initially planned to demand for the removal of the standards, however, Pilate had annoyingly taken them down already. Instead, Boaz was going to demand for the release of the prisoners, but this rabbi was even better.

"What is a rabbi again?" Pilate asked. He directed his question and his contempt at Boaz.

"A priest," the translator said, translating what Boaz had said.

"Rabbi? We have no rabbi in custody."

The translator spoke. The denial caused the crowd to stir. A couple of men replied.

A temple priest and a guard led Caiaphas into the courtyard. He was dressed in a cloak and stood at the very back to avoid being recognized. He didn't want to rouse the anger of Pilate again.

"They say he was taken in the night from his followers," the translator said. "Taken in the night and held without trial."

"Is that right? Is he one of his followers?" Pilate asked, pointing directly at the man with his scepter.

After the translation, the Jew violently shook his head.

"He says he isn't one of the followers," the translator said.

"Is he sure he isn't a follower?" Pilate stared down at him with derision. "What is his name?"

The translator spoke again. The Jewish man became white and his mouth became dry.

"Are you his follower?" Pilate asked directly.

The Jewish man looked at the ground and then disappeared into the crowd.

"We don't arrest rabbis," Pilate said. "Are they sure they don't mean their messiah?"

The translator spoke and the crowd began to quiet down.

"I'm not as familiar with the customs here. What is a messiah?" Pilate asked.

The translator spoke. The men's eyes in the crowd became very large and they began whispering to each other in a quiet panic.

"Ah, yes, I remember now. The messiah is supposed to restore the temple. The messiah is supposed to take his place at the head of the city. A king. Is that right?" Pilate was no longer playful but angry. As he said the word 'king', he seemed to almost spit in anger. The translator spoke and the mob shrunk back.

"We don't have rabbis, but we do have messiahs. Which one is your messiah? By all means, commander, bring them their king." Pilate motioned with his hands without taking his eyes off the crowd.

The commander escorted the torn and mangled prisoner onto the terrace in front of the governor. He was half-dead from the beatings and looked as though he had been put through a meat grinder. He had been beaten with fists and clubs. His back was bloody and mangled from being scourged by a flagellum, a three-foot-long whip with several thongs. Each strand was weighted with bone, nails, and lead to lacerate and tear the flesh away from bones. The blood was still pouring out and pooling at his feet.

Thorns had been twisted into a crown and had been forced onto his head. The skin on his face was pale and covered in blood.

The purple tunic Herod had given Pilate was draped over him. Boaz recognized the garment immediately. He and the crowd fell silent and still. They were frightened and disgusted at seeing the gruesome body.

While everyone could see the crucified bodies on the crosses outside the gates, most didn't make a habit of approaching them closely. This was a cruelty and humiliation they hadn't really seen in such detail. It was one thing to die quickly from a Roman soldier's spear. To be crucified was another matter altogether.

The once confident and stirring crowd was now docile and scared. The sound of plaster knocked to the floor by the wind could be heard.

Caiaphas was sick by the sight of a fellow Jew being tortured and humiliated. Yet he knew this was the outcome of Herod's and Boaz's challenge to Pilate's authority. This was the outcome of any challenge to Rome. He didn't dare say anything. This prisoner wasn't just a victim, he was a threat to the crowd.

"Here are your people, your majesty," Pilate said, giving a mocking bow.

The crowd became statues. Many Jews in the rear of the courtyard tried to leave through the gate, only to be blocked by the spears of Roman soldiers.

"Here is your king. You're his followers? Is this not the king you wished to recognize?"

The bolder men in front were angry and began to yell back at Pilate in disgust and outrage. Before the translator could speak, the angry men were quickly silenced by their scared friends.

After seeing their rabbi in such a disgusting condition, they tried to keep any other man in the crowd or their families from the same fate. They began to argue and yell at each other. They wilted as they imagined themselves or their families dying on a cross.

"What are they saying?" Pilate asked the translator.

"They are arguing. These ones in front want to speak out and their friends are trying to get them to be quiet."

"No need to be quiet. Speak up. What should be done with your king?"

As the crowd watched and whispered, the tortured prisoner swayed and stumbled, almost too weak to stand. The crowd stood rigid and silent. Then one of the men in the crowd yelled.

The translator spoke to Pilate. "They argued and then that one said they have no king but Caesar."

Boaz turned his neck toward the man so hard it almost snapped. Pilate couldn't resist a smile.

"Is that right?" Pilate said. "Well, it is terrible for them to come all this way and get nothing. Bring out another, commander."

The commander waved his hand and a soldier brought out a slightly-bruised man and positioned him next to the tortured rabbi.

"I will make you beggars a deal. I will release one of these men. Which should it be?"

The translator spoke. The followers in the crowd were arguing and shifting uncomfortably. It was very emotional and important to them, yet Pilate had a large smirk on his face. He smoothed out his cape and winked at Iovius.

"What has this other man been arrested for?" Pilate called out.

"Murder, sir," the commander said.

"Murder? That's a serious crime. Even by your barbarian standards. This should be an easy choice; a murderer or your king."

The mob had no answer. A few people began to cry, others covered their faces. Many tried again to leave but were stopped by the Roman soldiers boxing them in. The governor had not only shown them the torture that had been committed but was trying to make the crowd complicit in it.

"I will give them a few moments to decide." Pilate turned to enter the building. The translator spoke as he and his guards followed the governor.

Pilate entered his chamber with the messiah in tow. He walked over to a table and opened his wax tablet. He made a few small notes about water logistics from the aqueduct for later and wiped the small wax shavings onto the floor with his palm. He paced the room like an angry bull behind a fence. He struggled to rub the wax from his fingers. Eventually, he used the water from a basin against the wall to wash it off his hands.

On Pilate's orders, the commander draped a dirty cloth over the messiah and patted it against his back. The cloth turned from brown to black as it absorbed the blood.

Pilate was anxious to return to the crowd but he wanted to give them time to think about what they had seen. He wanted them to think about the blood and the pain. He wanted them to imagine themselves enduring the horrors of crucifixion.

"Are you their king?" Pilate asked the prisoner sarcastically. Pilate was very pleased with himself. He grinned and beamed at the soldiers and Iovius, who were compelled to laugh.

"You say so," the Galilean prisoner said in Greek.

The room became silent.

How dare this barbarian speak to me, he thought. Pilate turned back to him, shocked that he could even speak, let alone speak Greek. Wait, how does he know Greek? The governor rushed at him, stopping inches in front of the barbarian's nose. Pilate looked him in the eyes. They were half-closed from the swelling and bruising. It was the first and last time Pilate, or any other Roman, looked a Jew in the eyes. There was a brief moment when Pilate looked as if he could see something in his eyes, but it was quickly dismissed. He marched outside, raising his arms to the gathered Jews.

The commander grabbed the dirty cloth he had plastered on the messiah and ripped it away with one sweep of his arm. The clotted blood had glued the body and fabric together. As it was pulled away it tore the man's skin and blood began to flow. The commander pushed him outside onto the balcony.

Pilate watched the crowd look at the red and purple body of the prisoner. The confident and angry crowd now looked on in disgust and humiliation with large wet eyes. Pilate observed a completely different Jewish crowd. They were no longer agitators but scared whispering subjects trying to escape with their lives. No one was willing to suffer the same horrible fate.

"You've had time to think? Who should I release? This murderer? Or your messiah?" Pilate asked, folding his hand over his chest.

The crowd spoke.

"They say to release this man," the translator said, pointing to the murderer.

Pilate put his hand to his mouth in obsequious shock.

"Not their king? You don't want your king? "What crime has this other prisoner committed again?"

"Murder, sir," the commander said.

"Murder! You would rather I release a criminal, a murderer, than your king?"

The translator began to speak. Pilate put his hand up as he leaned into the crowd, descending the stairs like a charging elephant.

"Shut up, they can understand me! Are they sure they don't want their king? Boaz! Are you sure? You stand down there with them. Pathetic. If he really is your king, you should be scourged and crucified along with him. You're weak and low. Perhaps with your king, you could destroy all your enemies and take up residence in a palace built with the bones of your opposing army! Look at me when I say this. I will burn this city down and put each and every one of you on a cross like your king. You don't want standards around the city, very well. You want to have your religious nonsense, very well. But do not think for one moment I won't scourge the next person who stands outside my palace and demands something from me. Now, point, you beggars. Who am I to crucify?"

The crowd, like frightened children, slowly and silently pointed at the prisoner from the Galilee. Caiaphas looked away. He couldn't bear to see these people struggle to stop themselves from weeping. He knew Pilate would keep his post as governor. And as a result, Caiaphas would keep his post as high priest. The high priest was relieved yet afraid. Above all, he was disgusted. He was disgusted that he was indeed a Roman collaborator, just as Boaz had accused him of being.

Pilate waved his hand dismissively and smirked. "Let these animals leave with their shame," he yelled out.

The men in the courtyard slowly and carefully filed out onto the street. They passed by the Roman troops, looking at the ground. Each one hoped that if they didn't look up, then they wouldn't be the next to be scourged. Fear and terror gripped their hearts as they filed into the crowded Jerusalem streets.

The courtyard was empty except for Boaz. He stood alone, looking up at the Roman governor. Boaz knew he was in no danger, but he had lost. He had lost and had no choice but to report to Herod that there were no casualties and no problems managing the population. They were stuck with the poison of Rome and its governor.

Pilate lifted his hand and casually shooed him away.

"Hail Caesar," Pilate whispered to Boaz.

Pilate spun around, his cape flapping. The commander took the prisoner and tied the crossbar to his arms, leading him away to be crucified outside the city walls.

As Pilate reentered the palace, his face was flushed with excitement. He searched the room to see Iovius trying to stay out of sight behind two soldiers.

"Iovius. Now that is taken care of, let's discuss percentages."

"That's alright," Iovuis said. He was flustered and quiet. "We can wait until you're not so busy. Perhaps I should travel to Caesarea and meet you there when you will have more time."

"Nonsense," Pilate said. "Shall we have a bath?"